Murder
in the
Marsh

Murder in the Marsh

First Edition.
ISBN-13: 978-0-9863252-2-9
ISBN-10: 0-09863252-2-8

Copy edited by Marcus Trower.

www.adamfletcherseries.com
www.sarawhitford.com

SEAPORT
PUBLISHING

Printed in the U.S.A

"This place — Carteret County — this will always be home. And there's no place else I'd rather be."

— Adam Fletcher

MURDER
IN THE
MARSH

Sara Whitford

Chapter One

"Maybe she won't be too much longer, Aunt Celie." Adam Fletcher stood with hands folded in front of him at the base of the oak staircase and smiled at Aunt Celie. The fiftysomething-year-old slave woman was sitting in the foyer of the house in a ladder-back chair beside a trunk that was almost as big as she was.

She gave him a single small nod and a reserved smile. "Mmm-hm." She turned her attention back to watching the balcony on the second floor to see when her young mistress would appear again from the bedroom. Celia Martin—or Aunt Celie, as she was affectionately known—had a medium-brown complexion with few wrinkles. She was neatly dressed in a rose-colored, tailored gown, and her hair was pulled up under a matching cloth that was wrapped around her head sort of like a turban.

Adam felt nervous waiting there with the woman who was probably the single most important person in Laney Martin's life. Aunt Celie had been Laney's nursemaid as a baby. She had taken care of her and been her constant companion throughout her life. Laney and Will's mother, Alice, had died when they were children, and Celie had always been especially protective of Laney, looking out for her as if she were her own child.

After a few awkward moments of silence, Adam leaned on the curling, polished banister and called upstairs, "Miss Laney? You need help with anything?"

Within seconds the lovely young woman with honey-blond hair and green eyes leaned over the upstairs balcony. "I'm so sorry. I promise not to be much longer. Just trying to make sure I have everything packed."

"Well, if you need me, just holler and I'll be right up," replied Adam.

Aunt Celie raised her eyebrows in surprise, then turned her head away, but said nothing. She didn't have to. Her well-timed reaction said enough to make Adam feel even more nervous standing around waiting, and feeling nervous was not something to which the generally confident eighteen-year-old was accustomed.

It suddenly dawned on him that the old woman may have misunderstood his intentions, and that made him feel embarrassed. All he meant was that he would be happy to come up and help Laney get her things packed up and brought downstairs if she required assistance.

He should have known better than to think that Aunt Celie would be anything but wary about him going upstairs to be alone with the young lady. If Laney really did need help, Aunt Celie would be the one to give it, not him. The only reason the old woman was even sitting downstairs was because Laney had insisted Aunt Celie wait in the foyer and spend some time visiting with Adam while she was getting the last of her things together.

Visiting with Adam? Hardly. To Adam, the old woman was quiet as a church mouse and seemed nearly impossible to draw into conversation. She wasn't unfriendly towards him—not in the least—but she seemed determined to maintain propriety. Many would have thought it out of line for a Negro slave woman to engage in casual conversation with a free white man.

Adam figured she must have no idea how much he would appreciate her talking to him at this time, or any of the other times he had been to Laney Martin's estate, but he assumed she had decided to err on the side of caution by not speaking to him unless asked a direct question. On the other hand, Adam knew for a fact that she could say plenty when she wanted. Laney had told him there were several times when Aunt Celie had given her a good talking-to about one thing or another. While she always maintained the societally acceptable demeanor in public, at home she had rightfully exercised her role as both Laney's de facto guardian and mother figure since she was a little girl, not to mention she was the young woman's elder, even if she was *technically* a slave.

There was quite a bit of racket coming from upstairs.

Adam looked at Aunt Celie and raised his eyebrows in confusion. "I feel like I might ought to go up there and give her some assistance," he said, "but I don't know that it'd be appropriate."

The old woman looked at him thoughtfully. She seemed as if she wanted to say something but wouldn't, so Adam decided to be more direct.

"Do you think I should just go up there and see if she needs help, Aunt Celie?"

She pressed her lips together, then finally spoke. "I don't reckon that's called for, Mr. Adam. If Miss Laney need a thing in the world, she know Ima be right here."

Adam smiled at her, then nodded. "Indeed. You're absolutely right."

Just then the two of them looked across the room, as they could hear someone enter through the door on the north side—the riverfront side—of the house. Before Adam could say anything, Martin Smith came through the swinging door from the hallway into the foyer. The devilishly handsome blond-haired twenty-eight-year-old waved at Adam, then looked at the old woman and waved.

"Good mornin, Aunt Celie. You doin alright? All ready to go?"

"I'm just fine and I'm all ready, Mr. Martin," she said, tapping on the trunk next to her. "We just waitin on Miss Laney now."

"What in the world is takin that girl so long?" Martin directed his question at Adam. "There ain't nothin here that her brother don't have in New Bern!"

Adam shrugged. "I don't have the foggiest idea. She's makin all kinds of noise up there, though. I was just asking Aunt Celie if she thought I ought to go up and help, but..."

Martin chuckled, then gave Adam a sideways smile. "I reckon you did ask about going upstairs!" He looked over at the old woman and grinned. "What'd you tell him, Aunt Celie? He'd have to get past you first, right?"

Aunt Celie narrowed her eyes and gave Martin a sideways

stare, then let out a little giggle. "You know not! You know I wouldn't say no sucha thing, Mr. Martin!"

Martin flashed his blue eyes at her and winked. "Aw, I'm just teasin you, Aunt Celie. Just havin a little fun with you."

"Oh you!" She waved her hand at him dismissively and appeared to try to stifle a snicker.

Even though Martin Smith was Laney Martin's cousin and thus an extended member of the Martin family, it wouldn't have mattered. If anyone outside the estate could've gotten Aunt Celie to talk or laugh, it would be him.

Adam was grateful for it. It lightened the mood.

Martin leaned across the banister near where Adam stood and yelled upstairs, "Laney Martin! What in the world is takin you so long? We *got* to get goin, girl!"

Laney appeared over the balcony again. "I think I've got everything packed now. Just help me get this thing downstairs." She pointed towards her bedchamber, then started to come down the stairs. "It's just my old trunk," she told Martin and Adam. "That's all I'm bringing."

She came down to the foyer carrying only her little purse. It was made of green velvet that matched her emerald-green brocade dress perfectly. Adam was impressed with the way the color of her dress reflected the color of her eyes.

As she got to the bottom step, she said, "If y'all would get that for me, I'd be grateful."

Adam and Martin both ran up the stairs to Laney's room.

As soon as they got up there, Adam saw the trunk and looked at Martin. "What in the world does she have in this thing?"

Martin shook his head. "Don't ask me. There ain't a thing here for her to pack that her brother don't already have at his house in New Bern, except for her clothes."

Adam and Martin each grabbed an end of the trunk, which standing upright was nearly five feet high.

Adam said, "I don't see how a person can have enough clothes to fill a trunk like this."

"Well," said Martin, "if anybody would have enough clothes to fill a trunk like this, it would be my cousin."

Adam briefly considered the fact that aside from the clothes he was currently wearing—a dark-blue frock coat, a waistcoat in charcoal gray, a white shirt and cravat, and gray breeches—his entire wardrobe would easily fit in a small sack.

WHEN THEY FINALLY GOT THE trunk downstairs, they loaded up both Laney's and Aunt Celie's luggage and then assisted the two women onto the periauger for the two-day sail to New Bern. The ladies were planning to stay in the colony's capital through the winter, and with a string of Indian summer days, this would be a good chance to make the journey a pleasant and safe one.

Adam untied the boat from the dock, and Martin took his place at the tiller.

All of a sudden Aunt Celie grabbed Laney's hand and squeezed it. Laney looked at her, brow wrinkled in confusion, as it to say, *What is it?*, and the old woman leaned over and whispered, "Ain't they gon' pray?"

Laney did not hesitate to speak aloud Aunt Celie's concern. "Don't you say some kind of blessing before these voyages?"

"Voyage?" Martin chuckled. "We ain't goin to the Caribbean, girl—just New Bern!"

"Perhaps the two of you sail around so much you just take it for granted that you'll arrive safely, but it's not something we do every day, so we'd both appreciate it if one of you—as a gentleman—would say a word before we begin our travels. Otherwise, I'll just do it."

Martin rolled his eyes at Adam. He obviously thought it was ridiculous. Adam looked back at him in chastisement, then said to Laney and Aunt Celie, "You're absolutely right, ladies. We oughtn't take for granted that we'll arrive safely—even though we usually do. You never know if you might run into foul weather all of a sudden, or other sorts of troubles while traveling. I'll pray for us right now."

And he did. They all bowed their heads, and Adam offered a simple prayer that they would make it safely to New Bern without incident, and that he and Martin would have a safe journey back to Beaufort when it was time for them to come home.

Martin looked over at his cousin and said, "Are we ready now?"

Laney glanced beside her at Aunt Celie. The old woman then gave a nod.

Laney looked at her cousin and gave a single nod. "Yes, all ready now." She then turned her attention to Adam. "Thank you for the prayer."

Adam smiled at Laney. "Of course."

* * *

IT REALLY WAS A BEAUTIFUL day for sailing. They traveled up Core Sound, since the waters were calmer there than they would be offshore.

As they made their way north towards the Pamlico Sound, the four travelers spent time talking about all kinds of things. Adam shared colorful tales about unruly patrons that he had encountered over the years growing up in the Topsail Tavern. Martin told stories about his coworkers back at Rogers's warehouse, including some that had been particularly amusing to Adam when he'd first heard them. Laney told funny anecdotes from when she was much younger and her brother still lived at home, and she was able to draw Aunt Celie into the conversation by asking her to recall some of the occasions where Old Charles had saved the day, including one episode when Charles discovered Will had set a small fire on the lawn by holding a glass over some dry leaves in the noon sun and, quick thinking as he was, grabbed Aunt Celie's mop bucket and ran outside and dumped it on the small flames, getting young William wet in the process.

Concerning very practical matters, the ladies were initially apprehensive about how they would answer nature's call on board the periauger. They quickly figured out, however, that either of them could make use of the pot that was kept under one of the benches while the other stood in front of her holding up a blanket to offer her privacy. When they were done, they simply emptied the contents overboard.

Fortunately for Adam and Martin, they were easily able to stand and take care of their personal business right off of the side of the boat.

Late that night they made it as far as Cedar Island. Adam was relieved, as that meant, barring any unexpected weather conditions, they should be able to sail westward overnight down the Neuse River and arrive at New Bern a little after noon the next day.

Although he and Martin had been to New Bern a number of times on errands for Emmanuel, he had never been to Will Martin's estate. He was looking forward to seeing what it was like. In fact, this whole outing was something that had preoccupied Adam ever since he became aware they would be making the trip. It was the first time he had ever spent such a long stretch of time with Laney. He was grateful for a chance to have a longer visit with her than the usual few minutes of chatting that they were able to enjoy when they either ran into each other in town, or he had to go to her estate on business for Emmanuel.

He knew she liked him. At least he was pretty sure she did.

Ever since he had exposed the plot with Rasquelle and Reading the previous year—freeing her from the bonds of her unscrupulous guardian and protecting her from a potentially very dangerous situation—she had been especially friendly to him. At the end of that whole episode, she had gone so far as to call him her hero. He never did forget that, and even though he realized she was speaking only about that moment and those circumstances, in his heart he wanted to always be a man she could count on to look out for her and to protect her.

It wasn't just that, though. Adam knew a few things about young women. He had always been confident around them and had made more than his fair share of girls blush with just a well-timed wink or a smile. Back in the days when he thought his future would be centered around working at the Topsail Tavern, he assumed his dark, handsome looks, along with his self-assured personality, would be the virtues that would win him a bride—when he was ready to settle down, that is. And that was the last thing on his mind the day he was hauled down to the magistrate's office and bound in service to Emmanuel Rogers until his twenty-first birthday.

He was taken in by Laney Martin's beauty—and that laugh—the day he first met her at a party. It was as though he were a fish and she held the line, and now, more than a year later, he was still happily on that hook. As he came to know her, though, he realized she was even more beautiful inside than out. She was kind, headstrong, and independent—and able to take care of herself, but also sincerely cared for others. He found himself deeply attracted to her and wanting to be the man she chose to spend her life with.

Many of the single young women he knew in Beaufort (not that there were many—it was a small town, after all) were mild mannered and sweet natured, but they were for the most part just waiting for a suitor to come along and help them escape the monotony of life with their brothers and sisters, or to get out from under the authority of their parents. Laney, on the other hand, was orphaned as an adolescent, and though she had been assigned a legal guardian, he wasn't always around. Aunt Celie had been the closest thing she had had to a parent, and as a slave—even though she was very maternal to Laney—she still would not have expected to wield any legal authority over the girl. Any obedience Laney had to Aunt Celie had come out of her deep affection and respect for the old woman rather than any societal expectations. That spoke volumes to Adam—that she was compassionate and did not act spoiled or entitled, as other young ladies in her circumstances might have done.

That night, as they sailed across the sound without as much as saying a single word, Laney took the shawl that she had been using as a pillow and draped it over Aunt Celie. She could apparently see that the old woman was shivering, so Laney was trying to make her more comfortable. Adam knew there would be few women who might do that for another, much less for a slave, but that was just typical Laney. As quickly as she had taken the shawl and draped it over the old woman, Laney put her head down on her arms and tried to go back to sleep.

As they neared the mouth of the Neuse River, the wind died. That left Adam and Martin with little choice but to row the periauger if they hoped to continue moving towards their destination. Adam only hoped they could make it to New Bern sooner rather than later before a new wind came up out of the northwest, which would make them have to tack the last eighteen miles into the wind.

* * *

WHILE THEY HAD THOUGHT THEY should arrive around noon the next day, the journey up the Neuse was slow going. They finally approached the colonial capital around eight o'clock that night, and Martin led them to dock the periauger at a wharf near the peninsula between the Neuse River and the mouth of the Trent River.

"About how far is it to your brother's place?" Adam asked Laney.

Laney looked around to gauge exactly where they were. "Oh, we're actually quite close. They're just a few blocks north of here."

"Hmph." Adam was pleasantly surprised. "That's not far at all."

"It's too far for us to walk in the dark, though, and especially not with all our things." Laney looked at her cousin. "Why don't you run on over there and let them know we're here? You can come back with the cart."

"Sounds good," Martin agreed. "I'll be back directly!" He soon disappeared into the night.

Adam loved visiting New Bern. It was a bigger and busier town than Beaufort, and to him it seemed like a place where so much more was happening. The waterfront especially remained busier after nightfall than the one to which he was accustomed. In spite of not being the official customs port, New Bern received far more shipping vessels than Beaufort, thanks to the waterways that stretched far inland from the Neuse and Trent Rivers and their tributaries. When merchant ships arrived in the colony, it was much easier for them to forgo a trip to Beaufort and instead deliver their cargo directly to the capital. From there, other traders could arrange to carry any imported merchandise and commodities to all of the little inland towns that were situated along the tributaries of the Neuse. That strategy was much more effective for efficient deliveries than requiring merchant ships to stop in Beaufort first before traveling back up towards Ocracoke Inlet and then across Pamlico Sound to New Bern.

In less than half an hour Martin returned to the vessel in a horse carriage being driven by a handsome young man with a dark-brown complexion and closely cropped hair.

"Look who I found!" Martin exclaimed as they neared the dock.

They brought the carriage around to the front of the dock so that the back could be loaded with the luggage on board the boat. The driver of the carriage hopped down and enthusiastically strode over towards where the others were waiting.

"Mama!" he said, arms out wide.

Aunt Celie looked up at the young man and held out her arms as she ran towards him. "Oh, my baby!" she exclaimed.

The mother and son held each other in a warm embrace for a moment before Charles Jr., keeping his arm around his mama's shoulders, spoke to welcome the others to New Bern.

"I'm glad y'all finally made it. We was wonderin if it'd be tomorra 'fore y'all showed up. Mr. Will and Miss Catherine been lookin for y'all to get here all day. They been worried 'bout y'all. They was so happy when Mr. Martin here came ringin on that bell outside the house."

"We're glad we made it in tonight as well," said Adam. "I know these ladies will be happy to sleep in real beds. Last night was cold out on the water, and trying to rest in this old boat was challenging for these two. Still, I'll admit they bore the less-than-comfortable accommodations with grace."

"Is that right?" said Charles Jr. with a smile. "Well, let's just get y'all loaded up."

He walked over and appeared to notice the two trunks. It was easy to guess the smaller one belonged to his mother, but he still acted surprised by its size as he and Adam lifted Laney's larger trunk into the back of the carriage.

"Mama! What you bring in that trunk of yours? It ain't like y'all's movin here or nothin."

Aunt Celie wrinkled her brow and pressed her lips together as she dismissively waved at her son. "Oh! You just hush now, child! You know I had to bring my things if I was gon' be stayin here with y'all for the next month and a half! How am I s'posed to cook for all y'all children if I ain't got my things?"

Laney gave a knowing look to Charles Jr., who was rolling his eyes, and laughed at their exchange. She took Aunt Celie by the arm and walked her over to the door of the carriage, where Martin was waiting to give them both a hand. Laney insisted Aunt Celie climb in first and then she climbed in herself.

As Aunt Celie got into the velvet-lined carriage and took her seat, Charles Jr. looked in and said, "Don't you know the Martins have they own pots and pans? They got they own cook, Mama! You ain't come here to cook for Christmas!"

If looks could kill, Charles Jr. would have been dead right there in the street, for his mama looked at him like he needed to be quiet if he knew what was good for him. "You talkin mighty big, boy," she said. "You just quit runnin your mouth and showin off and take us on to Mr. William's place."

Charles Jr. didn't say another word and instead just climbed up in his seat to drive the carriage.

Adam's eyes grew big in amusement as he looked over at Laney's and Martin's reactions to the little scene. Apparently, Charles Jr. and Aunt Celie fussed just like he and his own mother did. It seemed to be a universal truth that sons often thought their mothers were being overprotective and ridiculous, while mothers always wanted to be prepared for any circumstance.

Martin and Adam took their seats in the carriage, and they were soon on their way to Will and Catherine's home.

Chapter Two

ADAM PAID CLOSE ATTENTION TO the route they were taking to get to Will Martin's estate. The lamplit streets were lined with all manners of houses, from palatial brick homes to small log cabins.

Fortunately, it was mostly a straight shot from the waterfront. They only had to ride about a block north to Pollock Street, then three blocks west until they reached Metcalf Street, at which point they turned right and then right again into the circular drive in front of the Martin home.

As soon as they stopped the carriage in front of the house, Will and Catherine, who was beginning to show the slightest swollen belly from the child she was carrying, stepped outside on the front porch to greet them.

"Thank God you all made it," said Will. "We've been anxious for you to arrive."

"Thankfully, we've had good weather," said Adam, "though it feels like the weather is about to turn."

He went around back to help Charles Jr. unload the trunks, while Martin assisted the ladies in exiting the carriage.

Will hugged his sister and then put his hand on Aunt Celie's shoulder. "I'm so glad you agreed to come by boat, Aunt Celie. I just heard earlier today about an incident that happened to a couple of travelers south of the Trent River. Terrifying story, and I'd have been a nervous wreck, I'm sure, if I had to worry about you two coming along that same path."

Aunt Celie glanced at Laney, then glared at Martin as if to say, *And you thought I was being foolish to want to pray for a safe journey.* Martin shrugged as if to say, *What? I didn't know.*

After the Martins welcomed their guests, Will asked Martin and Adam if they would bring Laney's trunk inside, and he gave Charles Jr. leave to help his mother take her trunk to his quarters.

"Where we goin?" Aunt Celie asked her son.

Adam could see that she looked concerned about not being in the main house with Laney.

"Oh, Aunt Celie, don't you worry," said Will. "We'll look after Laney while y'all are here. You just enjoy a nice visit with your son. You'll stay in his house."

Aunt Celie raised her eyebrows in surprise but didn't say a word. Instead, she looked in Laney's direction, as though she was seeking her approval of the arrangement.

Laney smiled at the old woman and nodded enthusiastically. "I'll be fine here, don't worry. I'll see you in the morning."

Aunt Celie nodded. "Alright, child. Don't forget to say your prayers."

"I won't," Laney warmly assured her. "I promise."

At that, Aunt Celie followed her son as he carried her trunk in a wheelbarrow to his quarters.

Adam was curious about where Charles Jr. lived on the Martin estate, since the family's slaves, Aunt Celie and Old Charles (when he was still living), stayed in a room in the main house at Laney's estate, while the two younger servants—both free Negroes—stayed in a small cabin adjacent to the barns. Adam noticed a small clapboard house just beyond the garden behind the main house with smoke coming out of a little chimney and a warm glow filtering through the foggy glass of the windows. It looked much cozier than the servant quarters at Laney's place—as though it had had a woman's touch to make it more homelike. Adam wondered if Charles Jr. was married, but he didn't think now was the time to ask.

As he and Martin were welcomed into Will and Catherine's home, Adam looked around and observed all that he could in the subdued light emanating from the lanterns of the foyer. From what he could see, most of the house was dark, with the exception of the room they were standing in, the nearby dining room, and what he assumed were two bedrooms upstairs.

"I imagine you all are hungry," said Catherine.

"We sure are!" said Martin.

Adam was glad he said it. He was ravenous and desperately wanted something warm to eat or drink. The cold food and drink on the boat, while enough to stave off real hunger, still didn't do much to satisfy.

"I guess y'all ate already," said Laney.

"We did, dear," said Catherine, "but we were only just fin-ishing up when Martin arrived to let us know you were here. We had Annabelle leave some dishes by the fire so we'd have something warm to feed you when you got settled in."

"Yes," said Will. "Y'all go on upstairs and get cleaned up, and your supper will be on the table when you come back downstairs."

* * *

THERE WERE FOUR BEDROOMS IN the main house at the Martin estate. Will and Catherine slept in one. Another was an elegantly decorated bedroom with one large bed, best suited for a lady visitor. It would be Laney's room during her stay. The third bedroom, which was more sparse, had two smaller beds in it. Its only decoration was a painting on one wall of a ship on a stormy sea and a bureau next to the wall with a basin and pitcher on top. The fourth bedroom, Adam was told, was on the first floor and was also a lovely guest room, but was more drafty in colder months, since heat rises and the room was on the rear side of the house, with a large picture window overlooking the garden. The Martins kept that room closed off during cooler months, but it was where they preferred sleeping in the summertime.

Adam and Martin had each only brought a single satchel of clothes, just to freshen up for when they were in town. They took turns washing their faces at the basin, each examining his appearance in the looking glass on the dresser, then changed clothes before going downstairs to have supper.

Laney was already downstairs, sitting at the table with Will and Catherine, when Adam and Martin came into the dining room.

"Have a seat, gentlemen," said Catherine. She motioned to the empty side of the dining room table, then used a tea towel to take the warm plates from the hearth and put them on the place settings in front of the young men.

Laney had already been served, but she was clearly waiting for her traveling companions to have their food in front of them, and Adam could tell that she was hoping one of them would say grace. He quickly gave a prayer of thanks for the food, and for the hospitality of Will and Catherine Martin, and then the three of them hungrily began to eat.

"Mmm... This is wonderful!" said Laney as she somehow maintained her poise and good table manners while moving food quickly from her plate to her mouth.

Will chuckled as he observed his younger sister, then looked at his wife, who smiled in amusement. Adam and Martin were eating so quickly they barely took time to breathe, much less speak.

"My goodness," Catherine commented, "you boys eat as if you think someone's going to come along and take your dishes away!"

Martin didn't seem at all embarrassed by her observation, but Adam's cheeks went a little red.

"I'm sorry, ma'am," he said. "This really is very good, and it's so nice to have a hot meal after spending two days eating cold food on the boat. My compliments to the cook."

Catherine nodded. "We'll be sure to tell her. Wait until you see what she'll be making tomorrow evening."

"Sorry," said Martin, cheeks full of food. "We were planning on leaving first thing in the morning. We have work, you know."

Adam wished they could stay another day. Seemed to him it was a waste to have to turn right around and go back to Beaufort if they had an invitation to stay an extra day and night in New Bern—especially if they were going to get a delicious supper out of it.

He was relieved when Will said to Martin, "It's Wednesday

night. If you leave tomorrow, you won't get back until suppertime Friday. There'll only be Saturday left for this workweek, and I don't reckon Emmanuel is so busy in this season that he can't do without you for one more day. As long as you're back in time for church on Sunday, he'll be happy."

Martin cocked his head to the side, as if he was going to argue, but Adam agreed with Will.

"He's right. Emmanuel won't care if we're not back until Saturday evening. It'd be nice to spend some time here in town tomorrow… have a nice supper with your cousins before we go back home."

"Well, but the thing is—" Martin countered.

"The thing is what?" said Adam. "The only thing you've got to look forward to in Beaufort on Saturday night is getting into mischief."

"But the mischief is more fun on Saturday nights," said Martin.

"That's a poor reason to rush back to Beaufort, and in any case for it, barring poor weather, we should still make it back in plenty of time for you to enjoy your Saturday night on the town. I say we should stay."

"I agree with Adam," said Laney. "Just stay tomorrow. Go to the shops. You can see if they have anything new and unusual that might interest Emmanuel."

"That actually doesn't sound like a bad idea," said Adam. He worked hard not to grin at the fact that Laney seemed just as anxious for them to stay as he was.

Laney lifted her eyes to look at Adam and smiled, then turned her attention back to her cousin. "Exactly. Then you fellows can come back here, have a good supper, get a decent night's sleep, and leave for Beaufort first thing Friday morning."

Martin looked at Adam first, then Laney, like they had both lost their minds. "Shopping? No thank you."

Laney rolled her eyes.

"Popping into the shops doesn't sound like a bad idea to me," said Will, "but you boys also might be interested in stopping by James Davis's place."

Adam gave Will a quizzical look. "James Davis?"

"Yes. He has the print shop down at the corner of Broad and Front Streets—he prints books from time to time, but he also publishes the *Gazette*. You can probably find out about the latest news before anybody else back in Beaufort does."

Martin and Adam both grinned at that idea.

"I knew that name seemed familiar," said Adam.

"I reckon I could make some money with information I could get in a place like that," said Martin.

"How do you mean?" asked Laney.

"Some well-placed wagers, my lovely cousin," he replied. He shoveled the last bit of food from his plate into his mouth.

Catherine's eyes grew huge as she looked over at her husband. Will just shook his head and tried not to laugh at his roguish cousin's suggestion.

"You're such a pig, Martin," Laney said, shaking her head in disbelief.

"I've been called worse." Martin laughed, then wove his fingers together and put them behind his head and leaned back in his chair.

Adam grinned at Laney across the table. "You think that's bad? I could tell you some things about this fella that would turn you as red as a beet." He tore his roll in half and used it to mop up the gravy on his plate.

Martin kicked Adam under the table.

"I'm sure you could tell us all kinds of things," said Laney, "but I doubt I'd even want to know all the devious things my cousin gets into."

"Probably it's best that way," said Will. "You learn too much about Martin's activities, and you might be considered an accomplice."

Catherine rolled her eyes in amusement. "Oh, good heavens."

"Aren't you proud, my dear?" Will said to her. "What a fine family you married into!"

"Oh my, yes! Very proud," she said. "So proud, in fact, that I think it's about time for me to retire for the evening so you all can talk about how grand you are."

Since Adam, Martin, and Laney were finished with their supper, Catherine took their plates away and put them in a basin of water to soak until the next morning. She excused herself to go to bed and left the others to continue visiting.

After a couple of hours of chatting, they all headed to their respective bedrooms to sleep.

Chapter Three

As TIRED AS HE WAS, Adam struggled to fall asleep his first night in the Martin house. He couldn't tell if it was because he didn't exactly feel *at home* in his more-elegant-than-usual surroundings, or if it was because Laney was sleeping in the very next room. Nevertheless, at some point he must've dozed off—and he must've slept hard—because the next thing he knew he was roused by the sound of hammering, which seemed to come from just outside his window.

It took him a second to make sense of his surroundings and remember where he was. He then quickly grabbed his pocket watch, which was on the nightstand between the two beds, and checked the time. It was eight o'clock! He couldn't remember the last time he had slept so late. When he saw that Martin was still sleeping hard in the other bed, he was relieved to know that at least he wouldn't be the last one downstairs for breakfast.

There was a chill in the air, and Adam hated to throw off the covers to get out of bed. He had slept in his breeches but had left his shirt draped on the chair by the window the night before. Nevertheless, he pushed back the heavy quilts and looked out the window onto the back garden as he reached over to grab his shirt and pull it over his head. It appeared that Charles Jr. was performing some kind of repair on the gate of the garden fence.

He couldn't help but stand for a moment at the window to admire the Martin property. It was only about an acre lot, but the space was all being used efficiently. On the eastern edge of the lot was a barn and chicken coop. On the back side of the property stood Charles Jr.'s small cabin, which Adam had caught a glimpse of the night before. Between that and the main house was the kitchen garden and the detached kitchen. Smoke was coming from the chimney, and he could see the silhouette of a woman working just inside the doorway.

When he heard women's voices outside, he looked straight down from the window and saw Laney standing there talking to Aunt Celie about something. That woke Adam up enough that it dawned on him that he'd soon be going downstairs and would see not only Will Martin and his wife but Laney would be there.

He instinctively reached up and grabbed at his face and rubbed his chin and cheeks. He realized he now had nearly three days' growth of nearly black stubble, and at the rate his facial hair grew, that was far more than he wanted to have if he was going to be around Laney Martin or potentially conducting business in town.

Adam crossed the room to the dresser and looked in the oval mirror that was mounted on the wall above it. He tucked a piece of his dark-brown hair behind his right ear and turned his head from side to side as he observed himself.

Oh, Lord... I do look like him—especially today.

He was thinking about his father, Santiago. For eighteen years Adam never knew the identity of the man who had married his mother, then disappeared from Beaufort before he was ever born. But just four months earlier Adam had finally found the man—in Havana, Cuba of all places—and within days had to say good-bye to him, as he was suffering from the ever-worsening effects of a fatal gunshot wound. His father had begged him not to stay around to watch him die but to remember him as he was alive, so that was what Adam had done. But now that he was back in North Carolina, it was as if he saw Santiago's face almost every time he looked in the mirror. Especially when his stubble was creating a dark shadow that drew attention to his chiseled cheekbones. Adam's shoulder-length wavy, nearly black hair, tangled and hanging down around his face in the morning, seemed to double the effect.

Just thinking back on the short time he had with his father, Adam suddenly didn't care who saw him like this. He would just run a comb back through his hair and put it in a ponytail. That would have to be good enough.

He washed his face and finished getting dressed, then tapped at the foot of the bed where Martin slept to let him know he would be heading downstairs. Martin just mumbled something unintelligible, so Adam left him there.

As soon as he got downstairs, he saw Will and Catherine sitting at the dining room table, having breakfast.

"Good morning," he said to them.

Will invited him to sit down and eat, so Adam thanked him and took a seat.

"Where's my cousin?" Will asked.

Adam gave him a half smile. "He's still asleep. I tried to wake him. Maybe he'll be down soon."

Catherine offered Adam a cup of tea, then called into the adjacent room for someone named Annabelle to bring him breakfast.

A woman's voice from the other room responded, "Yes'm. Be right there."

After a moment or two a young servant woman of about Adam's age came into the room carrying a tray of food. Annabelle's light skin color and blue eyes, paired with exceedingly curly black hair, suggested she had mixed African and European heritage. She placed a plate of eggs and sausage, along with a bowl of grits, in front of Adam. She then asked Will and Catherine if they needed anything else. Catherine shook her head, so Annabelle took their dishes away.

After bowing his head to quickly say grace, Adam looked around the room as he started eating and observed, "Your home is beautiful. I was admiring your garden from the window upstairs. Seems a smart use of a small space."

Will chuckled. "Thank you. It was… well… different getting used to living here after being raised on my father's estate. To go from growing up on fifty sprawling acres to squeezing into less than an acre—it took some getting used to." He waved his hand to motion proudly at his wife. "But Catherine here was raised in the city, so she was very accustomed to making efficient use of a small plot."

"Oh really?" said Adam. He nodded and smiled as though he was finally understanding something that had been perplexing him. "I had suspected she wasn't raised around here." He turned his attention to Catherine. "Where did you grow up, Miss Catherine?" He continued eating.

Catherine gave a little laugh and said, "I suppose my manner of speaking must give it away."

Adam grinned but didn't say anything but "Mm-hmm," since his mouth was full.

"I was born in Boston," she said. "My father was a merchant—not unlike your master, Emmanuel Rogers, from what I hear."

Will raised his eyebrows in surprise and leaned back in his chair and looked at his wife. "Well, dear, Emmanuel is a merchant, yes, but your father's business was probably ten times as large as Rogers's Shipping Company—at least!"

Adam swallowed hard, and his eyes grew large as he looked from Will to Catherine. "Are you being serious?!"

"Of course I'm being serious," said Will. "Boston's a big city with a great population. Beaufort is just a small, inconsequential little town that in spite of being right near the ocean can't even attract merchant ships as easily as this town a full fifty or so miles from the sea!"

"Aw…" Adam shook his head. "Now that's not fair. You know as well as I do that Beaufort has the best harbor along the whole coast of this colony—better than even Wilmington! We can't help it that there are no rivers going inland from there. Beaufort would probably be as fine a port as Charleston—or Boston—if there were!"

Will chuckled and tipped his head in Adam's direction as he looked at Catherine. "This one was born and raised in Carteret County—and is sure proud of it, if you can't tell!"

Adam rolled his eyes.

Catherine looked like she was trying hard not to giggle. "Oh,

Adam! Don't pay him a bit of mind if he's making jokes about your home port! He forgets that I know *he* was born there, too— and I'm sure Beaufort is a lovely town." She looked teasingly at her husband. "Although Will has never seen fit to take me beyond the perimeter of his family's estate there."

Will shook his head. "I've told you, dear. There's really nothing to see in Beaufort. Just hogs running loose in the streets mostly—and we can see those sights right here in New Bern."

Adam stabbed one of the pieces of sausage on his plate with a fork, then held it up and grinned before taking a big bite. "How true! At least they're tasty little beasts!"

He couldn't help but laugh, particularly since just the night before Charles Jr.'s carriage had to stop for Charles Jr. to shoo away some hogs that were milling around in the street, eating some scraps that someone had thrown out. Will and Catherine laughed right along with him.

Just then Laney came into the dining room. "What are y'all cutting up about in here?"

"Oh, nothing really." Adam grinned. "Your brother was just talking about how the livestock that runs wild in the streets here in New Bern reminds him of home."

Laney made a disgusted face as she pulled out the chair next to her sister-in-law and took a seat. "You'd think things'd be more civilized here in the capital."

"You'd think so, wouldn't you?" Will agreed.

"Where's my lazy cousin?" Laney asked Adam.

Adam shrugged, then motioned upstairs. "Sleeping the day away, I reckon."

"Of course he is," said Laney. "Why did I even bother asking? I reckon he went on a drunk last night and he's sleeping it off this morning."

"Laney!" Will exclaimed, making it clear that he couldn't believe she'd say something so coarse.

Laney looked at her brother matter-of-factly and said, "What? You know it's the truth. Martin is happiest when he's dipped his bill!"

"Laney! I declare! That's enough!" Will sounded as though he was trying to chastise her, but he was too amused to come off as serious.

Catherine could barely contain herself, so as not to make the situation spiral into much silliness, she graciously excused herself from the room to go see if she could assist Annabelle.

Adam was shocked, but humorously so. He never thought he'd hear Laney use a phrase like that to describe a drunken state.

"Where in the world did you hear something like that?" he asked.

Laney leveled her eyes at him and said, "What? You think I don't pay attention when you boys are over on my dock for Emmanuel, unloading those *secret* shipments, running your mouths like y'all tend to do." She tapped her right ear with her fingertip. "I listen to y'all... Just you keep that in mind when you think you're having private conversations." She gave him a smile and a nod.

Adam raised his eyebrows and grinned at her. "Hmm... I'll have to remember that then, missy, and be careful what I say around you!"

Chapter Four

As soon as Adam finished with his breakfast, Laney said she wanted to go shopping, and Catherine agreed that it would be fun, so Will asked Adam if he and Martin wouldn't mind taking his carriage and dropping the ladies off in front of the shops over on Craven Street. He explained that he had to leave for a meeting with one of his clients about an estate sale, but it was in the opposite direction and he could easily walk to it, so it wouldn't make sense for him to take them.

Ordinarily, Catherine could've gotten Charles to do it, but he had other work to attend to that morning and had been promised the rest of the day off, since it was his mother's first day visiting. Adam was more than happy to oblige, but he'd have to wake up Martin first.

It was no small task, but finally Martin was up and fed, and they were on their way.

Craven Street was three blocks away from the Martins' home and only one block from the riverfront. There weren't many shops, but the ones that were there had a great variety of imported items. Beaufort had its imports as well, but not as many and not in such diversity as could be found in the New Bern shops.

Adam was interested in visiting the local merchants to see if there were any items he could suggest to Emmanuel, but he remembered what Will had said about James Davis's print shop— and he knew that had interested Martin—so they decided they would go there first while the ladies took their time browsing.

"Where are you boys from?" said Mr. Davis, a middle-aged man overseeing a young fellow of about sixteen as the boy banged the surface of the type on the galley with a pad of black ink.

Adam assumed the boy was the man's apprentice.

"Beaufort, sir," said Martin.

Adam was so fascinated with seeing a printing press in action for the first time that he hadn't paid much attention to the question.

"Are you here on business or for pleasure?" Mr. Davis asked.

"A little of both," Martin responded.

"You know," said Adam, without looking up from watching the young man blot ink on the type, "I've never seen anything like this being done before. How long did it take you to get that type arranged in that tray?"

The young man answered, "I'm not as fast as him yet, but it takes *hours* to get the typesetting done for just one page."

"I think it's fascinating," said Adam.

"I reckon you boys are here to check up on how Carteret

County's making out over in the General Assembly, eh?" said Mr. Davis.

"We came to see family here," said Martin.

"Well, depending on when you boys leave, you'll be able to take the news back before it makes it in the paper."

"What news?" asked Adam.

"Oh, you haven't heard? They're passing a piece of legislation, introduced by Mr. Richard Cogdell, that will see a canal built to connect Harlowe Creek to Clubfoot Creek. Beaufort port will have a direct waterway to the Neuse River."

Adam and Martin looked at each other in amazement.

"That's some good news!" said Martin. "When did they say they'll get started?"

"Hmm... not sure, but it'll be dependent on interested citizens. The Crown won't pay for it—not with Governor Tryon's new residence to be built. That'll cost a small fortune."

Adam and Martin stayed and chatted with Mr. Davis a while longer. They found him to be an interesting man, and as it turned out his wife's family had connections with the Martin family, which opened a whole different line of conversation. After nearly an hour they left and went back to the shops to pick up Laney and Catherine. They helped the ladies load up their parcels—of which there were several—and took them back to the house.

After that, Adam and Martin said they wanted to walk back down to the business district to look around. They declined Catherine's offer that they take the carriage, saying they wouldn't need it and that they would be back in a few hours.

Chapter Five

Adam returned to the estate alone late in the afternoon. Martin had stayed behind at a pub by the wharf but promised he'd be back to his cousins' house in time for supper.

When Adam came through the front door and into the foyer, he saw Laney and Will sitting in the parlor, which was to the right, just before the staircase, arguing. He could overhear their conversation.

"If I'd have known she would feel like this—if I'd have even *known* that she'd be getting hit with all of this news—I don't know that I'd have even brought her here."

Laney was visibly angry with her brother. Adam could tell she must have been talking about Aunt Celie, but he had no idea what had her so upset. He felt awkward walking in on what was clearly a family matter.

"I'm sorry," he said. "Excuse me."

He ducked across the foyer and past the entrance to the parlor quickly and started up the stairs.

"Adam, wait a minute," Laney called out. "I want to ask you a question."

Adam turned around and came back down the stairs and leaned his head into the room. He looked at her, hoping that her question didn't pertain to the argument she was having with her brother.

"I want to ask if you think I'm being unreasonable," said Laney just as sweetly as she could.

Adam took a deep breath, then looked apologetically from Laney to Will. He had nothing to be sorry about, of course. Laney was the one bringing him into their dispute, but still, if he hadn't entered the house at that particular time, he wouldn't have landed himself in the middle of their discussion.

"Laney," said Adam. "I don't have the foggiest idea what y'all are talking about. And I'd just as soon not get in the middle of whatever it is."

He smiled at her and hoped she'd let him go on about his business—which involved going to the room he was staying in upstairs and *not* participating in their argument.

Laney raised her eyebrows in disappointment and looked at him pleadingly.

Adam sighed. "I'm sure y'all can work it out—whatever it is."

He started to take another step upstairs when Laney called to him again. "Wait!"

He stopped and slowly turned around.

"Adam Fletcher," she said, "you always seemed to me to be a reasonable person. I'd like to have your opinion—as a neutral party. If you think I'm being unreasonable, I'll take your word for it and drop the matter... maybe." She looked at her brother.

Adam glanced over at Will again. He wondered if he shouldn't just go ahead and hear what Laney had to say so he could be excused from the situation.

Will tipped his head in his sister's direction and gave Adam a look as if to say, *Come on and help me put an end to her fussing.*

Adam reluctantly came back down the stairs but waited at the landing rather than going all the way into the room. He had no intention of staying in this discussion any longer than he absolutely had to.

"Alright," he said to Laney. "What is it you want to know?"

"Come in here," she insisted.

Adam obliged.

Laney began to make her case. "You know Aunt Celie has been an absolute mess since Old Charles died, and I brought her here so she could spend time with Charles Jr.—for the Christmas season—so it would make her happy."

Adam nodded. "Yes. It's nice that y'all both can come here and spend the holiday with your families."

"Well"—Laney took a deep breath before she began to spill out the details of her frustration—"Aunt Celie is anything but happy right now, because almost as soon as we got here she was informed that not only is her son getting married but that he's also worked out an arrangement with my brother to buy his freedom."

Adam's eyes grew large. He looked at Will. "Oh really? Well, that's great news!" Then he looked at Laney and said, "Why in the world is Aunt Celie upset?"

Will nodded in agreement with Adam. "Exactly! There's no

reason for her to be upset—and that's what I'm trying to explain to my sister."

"You're not a woman, and you're not a mother!" Laney said in exasperation. "I don't know why I would ever think you could understand something like this!"

"You're not a mother either," said Will.

"Yes, but as a woman I think I have a better understanding of these matters than you do. Aunt Celie thought she was coming here to spend time alone with her son, remembering Old Charles, and enjoying Christmas together. She was also looking forward to mothering him while she was here—cooking for him, cleaning for him, and so forth—but apparently Annabelle has already stepped into that role. And now she feels like he doesn't need *or* even want her to take care of him while she's here. She feels useless!"

Adam wrinkled his brow, unsure of what to say. No matter. Laney wasn't finished.

"And to make matters worse, this business about Charles Jr.'s emancipation has her worried to death!"

"She's being ridiculous about it," said Will.

Adam nodded in agreement. "I'd think she'd be happy about that. She really is upset?"

"Yes! She's fit to be tied!" said Laney. "Aunt Celie has never been fond of changes, and this is just too much change all at once. Not to mention no matter how much I try to tell her she needn't worry about emancipation changing anything for her or Charles Jr., she simply *cannot* be consoled."

"She doesn't want to be free?" Adam asked.

"I asked her the same thing," said Will, shaking his head. "She only ever says, 'What for?' She was born into our family— well, into our mother's family—and being a part of our household is all she's ever known. She knows we've always cared well for her and her family. They've never had to worry about being mistreated, and they have a certain amount of prestige with folks because they belong to us. She's afraid they'll lose that security if we manumit them."

"But surely it isn't like y'all are just going to turn them out in the street if you free them. She has to know that," said Adam.

"Oh, I've told her," said Laney. "I've told Aunt Celie I'd give her emancipation papers if she wanted them, but she says she doesn't care a thing about it. She doesn't want to work for anybody else, and she doesn't want to take money from me for her work. She says I'm like one of her own children, so she wouldn't feel right for me to pay her—that I already do by having her live in my house and making sure she has all the things she needs."

"So just tell her that you'll give her emancipation papers and then let her keep staying on with you as family," Adam countered.

"Don't you think I've told her I'd do that?" Laney argued, waving her hands around wildly. "I have! But she says there's no sense in giving her papers if she doesn't want to go anywhere else anyway. 'Why not leave things the way they are?,' she says."

Adam knew at this point there was nothing he could contribute to the conversation. He couldn't figure out why Laney wanted to bring him into it to begin with. He thought about excusing himself to go on upstairs, but an idea occurred to him, and he couldn't help but suggest it.

"Why don't you just go ahead and manumit Aunt Celie and then insist she stay with you? You don't need her permission to free her."

"You mean go behind her back and free her?" Laney twisted up her face in disgust. "She'd never forgive me! I'd have never thought that you of all people, Adam Fletcher, would suggest such a deceptive thing!"

"What's wrong with what he's suggesting?" said Will. "It makes perfect sense to me."

"No, it doesn't!" Laney disagreed. "It'd break her heart. I know Aunt Celie, and it would worry her to death that I'd turn her out... or that something would happen to me—in childbirth, for instance—and there would be no security for her."

"But you aren't even married," said Adam. "Aren't y'all putting the cart before the horse a bit worrying so far down the road?"

"You've seen how some folks treat Negroes," said Laney. "It's awful. I can understand how Aunt Celie would want to feel assured of the protection she has as a part of this family. I can also understand how she'd worry for her son, but why my brother would enter into an arrangement with Charles Jr. for him to *buy* his freedom—that's another issue altogether. I don't see why he doesn't just manumit him outright."

"I've told you, Laney," said Will, "Charles Jr. is working to buy his freedom, but I'm going to turn right around and give him that money back as a gift to help him establish himself as a freeman. He doesn't know that, but that's my plan."

"Well, let's get back to your question, Laney. You asked me if I thought you were being unreasonable, but I don't understand what is supposed to be unreasonable here. Who's saying you're being unreasonable? And about what?"

Laney lowered her head and pressed her fingertips against her forehead in exasperation before looking up to answer. "My brother thinks it's unreasonable that I'm upset that he didn't warn me about all of this before we came." She looked at her brother with angry eyes. "Because he knows if he had told me beforehand, we probably wouldn't have come at all."

"I think it would've been unreasonable for y'all to stay back in Beaufort all by yourselves over Christmas because you're too worried that Aunt Celie is going to have hurt feelings. Of course I didn't warn you about all of this. How would I? In a letter? I had no way of knowing how upset she'd be! And I thought she'd be happy Charles Jr. is planning to get married—and to a free-woman no less."

"I don't see how any of this matters now," said Adam. "What's done is done. I don't reckon Aunt Celie's heart would be as fragile if she weren't still mourning the loss of Old Charles. If she feels upset because Annabelle is doing all the cooking and cleaning for Charles Jr. right now, that's going to be something they're going to have to work out for themselves. I think Charles Jr. ought to let his mama cook for him at least. Mamas live for doing that kind of thing. I'm sure I can find a roundabout way to talk to him about that, since knowin my mama, she'd be just as bad."

"Would you, Adam?" Laney asked. "That might help a bit. If she can at least be able to do those simple things for her son, I think it would help. We can address the emancipation issues later."

Adam nodded. He looked at Laney and Will and then asked if he could be excused to get cleaned up before supper.

* * *

THE DINING ROOM TABLE WAS quite a sight. The room had been a common, if not high-end, eating space the previous two times Adam had seen it, but now it was transformed into a proper banquet room.

The table was dressed with a damask cloth and lace runner, along with fine china with full place settings. On the sideboard there were covered dishes of white-and-blue porcelain. When the lids were removed for Annabelle to serve each person around the table, Adam's mouth began to water. There was a standing rib roast, a deep dish of creamed potatoes, another filled with ham hock–seasoned snap beans with cornmeal dumplings, and another with stewed carrots. There was a large basket of rolls, a crock of butter, and for dessert there was a pear cobbler with a pitcher of fresh cream.

After everyone was seated and it seemed unlikely that Martin would show up on time, he stumbled through the front door of the house and scurried into the dining room.

Adam rolled his eyes at Martin, then shook his head, annoyed.

"What?" said Martin. "I said I'd make it for supper, and here I am—just in time it looks like."

"Honestly," said Laney, "you have the manners of a wild boar hog. Doesn't it embarrass you to come tumbling into a fine meal late like this?" She waved her hand over the fully set table and the sideboard.

"Embarrass me?" Martin feigned shock. "Why should I be embarrassed? Y'all are family. You ought to know not to expect much."

Will grimaced and looked at his wife. It seemed as if he was silently apologizing for having such unrefined relations.

"Just have a seat, Martin. We're about to give thanks," he said.

Martin scuffled over to the chair next to Adam and sat down.

Adam inhaled deeply but discreetly. He wanted to know whether it was just the initial whiff from when Martin sat down, or if the rascal really did reek of alcohol. No, it wasn't just a fleeting odor. Martin smelled like he'd been pickled in rum.

It was awkward for everyone. Nevertheless, Will said grace, and they all started eating.

For a few moments no one said anything. They were too busy chewing. Eventually, Martin spoke up.

"So, what have *you* heard about that murder that happened south of Clermont Plantation, Will?"

The mention of the murder piqued Adam's curiosity, but he bristled at his friend bringing up such a grisly subject at a fine meal, where he'd already pushed the limits of tolerable behavior.

Will first glanced at his pregnant wife, who appeared to grimace at the mention of a murder, then he wrinkled his brow and looked pensive as he chewed a mouthful of beef.

Maybe he's trying to decide whether or not to send Martin upstairs, Adam thought.

Will took a deep breath before answering. "A husband and wife were returning back to New Bern from visiting family out on Clubfoot Creek when they were accosted by two highwaymen. There was a struggle, and one of the two travelers lost his life. The other survived." Will lowered his eyes at his cousin and in a serious tone said, "I think that's enough of that kind of talk at the supper table. If you want to know any more, you can ask me about it after the ladies have retired for the evening."

"Fair enough," said Martin.

"I know what I'd like to talk about," said Will. "Adam, what's this I hear about you being Emmanuel Rogers's grandson?"

"I know it!" said Martin. "And how 'bout that? We're all grandsons of pirates, after all!"

Adam grinned proudly and nodded. "It came as a surprise to me. I found that out months ago. I hadn't thought about the fact that y'all wouldn't know about that yet."

"I mentioned it to him in a letter," Laney said to Adam, "but I told him it was a long story and that you could share it with him when you saw him."

"Aw, Laney," said Adam. "I'm touched that you would even

mention me in your correspondence to your brother." He gave her a wink.

She blushed and smiled, then quickly said, "Oh, of course I did! You know it was the biggest news after y'all got back from Havana. Who wasn't talking about it?"

"Mm-hmm." Adam grinned. Whether she had written it in a letter because it was local news or not, Adam still liked thinking that she thought enough about him to mention him to her brother.

"So tell me!" said Will. "What's all this about? How did you find out?"

"Well," said Adam, "your sister's right. It is a long story, and I don't know that all of it is appropriate for the supper table, but I'd be happy to tell you all about it later."

"Very good," said Will. "I'll hold you to that—but tell me, what did you think when you found out? And I hear you met your father as well!"

Adam nodded. "I did, but I don't know if you heard that I had barely gotten to know who he was when I lost him."

Will wrinkled his brow in sympathy. "Did you really? Oh, that's terrible. I'm so sorry."

Adam proceeded to explain the highlights of the story, without getting into any of the gruesome details. He told Will that he was thrilled to learn Emmanuel was his grandfather, especially considering he already thought so much of him as a master.

Catherine seemed to be especially moved by Adam's account and asked what his mother had thought about him finding his father, or learning of his fate.

"My mother was worried to death about me going to Havana, and I just couldn't understand it. I know for a fact she wouldn't have been quite as worked up if I'd have been going anywhere else, so obviously, when I learned her reasons, I realized why she was so concerned. Above all else she was just relieved that I made it home safe, and she was as surprised as I was about Emmanuel being my grandfather—especially since my father didn't even know."

"That's unbelievable!" Will commented. "You ought to write it all down. That's quite a story!"

Adam chuckled. "Ah, no. I don't think I'll be airing our family's secrets for all the world to read. This isn't exactly the kind of family history you want to brag about. I'm only telling you because y'all are like family, anyway. And it's not like I would hide that Emmanuel is my grandfather now that I know about it. Neither would he."

"Well, I for one think it's a beautiful, tragic story," said Catherine. "It sounds to me like your mother and father loved each other very much, and it's heartbreaking to think of how they were kept apart for so long."

Adam nodded and gave her a small smile. He didn't know what to say, though. Of course it was tragic. Of course it was heartbreaking. No one could imagine how he, or his mother, or father, or even Emmanuel felt or were impacted by all of the years of keeping secrets. He was just grateful that the truth was out now, though.

After the meal Laney and Catherine cleared the table, as they had dismissed Annabelle after dinner was served. Will invited Adam and Martin into the parlor for drinks and gentlemanly conversation, which mostly amounted to Will peppering Adam with questions all about his adventure in Havana. Martin had quite a bit to add as well now that the ladies were out of the room.

Will answered Martin's and Adam's questions about the murder that had been mentioned at the supper table.

"How did you find out about all of that?" said Adam. "Mr. Davis didn't say nearly as much down at the paper today."

"Ah well," said Will, "my good friend Alexander Pearce is the family's attorney. He knows all of the details firsthand from the lady victim. We never give all of the information to the papers, though. We wouldn't want to influence any possible witnesses."

"Very smart," said Martin.

The three of them sat up until nearly midnight talking, but Adam finally suggested they all get some sleep, as he and Martin would be leaving early the next morning to return to Beaufort.

Chapter Six

FIRST THING FRIDAY MORNING CHARLES Jr. took Adam and Martin to the wharf and wished them well on their journey back to Beaufort.

Adam remembered what he had told Laney and Will about speaking to Charles Jr., so he told Martin to wait a minute while he went over to the carriage to talk to him before he left.

"Listen," said Adam, "I wanted to mention something to you before we leave for Beaufort."

Charles Jr. seemed surprised as he looked at Adam. "What's that, Mr. Adam?"

"A little bird told me your mama is not real happy right now."

"Excuse me?" Charles Jr. seemed perplexed that Adam would be approaching him about his mother. "Whatchu mean, sir?"

"Well, from what I gather, seems she's sad because she came

all the way here and had it in mind to cook for you and clean for you and do all those things mamas like to do."

"Oh." Charles Jr. rolled his eyes. "I see. She's actin plain foolish. I told her I got Annabelle lookin after me now. She ought to just rest! When she's ever been able to do that, huh?"

"I understand what you're saying," said Adam, "but—"

"Goodness gracious! I try to do something nice and she still gon' holler about it!" Charles Jr. continued. "Ain't no need for her to be doin all that hard work!"

"That's the problem, though," said Adam. "Without anything to do, now she feels useless."

Charles Jr. pulled back his head and twisted up his face in shock. "Do what? Why she thinkin like that?"

Adam put his hand on Charles Jr.'s shoulder. "Come on now, Charles. You've got to know that mamas live for fussing over their children—even when we're grown. Trust me, I know. My mama raised me by herself, and she's the same way."

Charles Jr. put his hands on his hips and laughed as he seemed to consider the shared emotions of mothers and their sons, slave or free.

Adam gave him a look as if to say, *Trust me. I know what I'm talking about.*

Charles Jr. nodded in understanding. "I'll see if I can't make 'em both happy."

Adam smiled, then shook his hand and wished him well, then climbed back into the periauger. Charles Jr. waved at them and rode away.

"What was all that about?" Martin asked.

"Oh, just giving some son-to-son advice," said Adam.

He explained everything he had learned about Aunt Celie's

emotional turmoil. He then recounted the advice he'd given to Charles Jr.

"Aunt Celie's right to be worried about Charles Jr.'s emancipation," said Martin. "The safest place her or her son can be is sheltered under the wings of my cousins' family."

"I understand her worries," said Adam, "but there are plenty of free Negroes around. Don't you reckon they're a lot happier being free than they would be being slaves?"

"Sure," said Martin. "Some of 'em are, but also don't forget they've got to work a lot harder so they can afford all the things that they would just be given if they had masters."

"Work harder?" said Adam. "That's the stupidest thing I've ever heard! They already work their fingers to the bone *for* their masters, then they don't even get paid for that. I don't see how being free they have to work any harder. The only difference is they get to keep the fruits of their labor rather than it fattening their masters' coffers."

Martin made a face at Adam. "Tell me what it is that Aunt Celie *or* Old Charles *or* Charles Jr. is doin that's makin my cousins any richer. I don't see no tobacco plantations or cotton plantations in this family!"

"I know that," said Adam, "but still, don't you reckon it frees Will up to focus on his attorney's work with Charles Jr. doing the labor around his house?"

"Yes," said Martin. "And yet still my cousin plans to give him his papers. And then he'll hire him to do the same work as a freeman."

"Right," said Adam. "He'll get paid to do the same work he's been doing for free as a slave all of these years."

"Yes, but Charles Jr. will no longer be able to say he belongs to the Martin family, and since a Negro can't testify against a white person in court, what recourse would he have if someone did abuse him in some way?"

"Your cousin is an attorney, for goodness' sake," said Adam. "You don't think he'd seek justice for Charles Jr. if, God forbid, anything like that were to happen?"

"Of course he would," said Martin, "but Will might not always be around. Then what?"

Adam waved his hand dismissively at Martin. "Oh, this is a ridiculous conversation. You can't convince me that a slave has it better than a freeman."

"Not just any freeman," said Martin, "and not just any slave. I'm talking about a slave in *our* family versus a free Negro."

Adam decided to drop the conversation. He understood both sides of the argument, but no one could convince him that it was better to be a slave than to be a freeman—regardless of what family that slave belonged to. He was glad Will apparently agreed with him and had worked out that deal with Charles Jr.

The rest of the way back to Beaufort, they avoided the topic of Aunt Celie or slavery. Instead they talked about the news they'd learned at James Davis's print shop, including the bit about the canal, as well as the couple that had been attacked several days earlier.

Adam said he couldn't wait to get back to Beaufort and tell his grandfather about the canal plans. Martin said he couldn't wait to get back to Beaufort so he could go drinking with Ricky Jones.

Jones had been on the *Carolina Gypsy* when they went to Havana and wasn't usually in Beaufort for very long, but Emmanuel was having some substantial repairs done to the sloop, so Martin and Jones, as everyone called him, seemed to be trying to work in as much wild living and mischief as they could in the time that was available before Emmanuel sent Jones out again with the crew. Since Emmanuel knew all too well the kind of entertainment that Martin and Jones generally sought, he had put his foot down about allowing his grandson to go out carousing with the two of them.

As they sailed down the Neuse River out to the Pamlico Sound, they noticed the weather was getting colder. By the time they neared Cedar Island, they were grateful that they were on their return trip and only had about another twelve hours of sailing ahead of them—that was, if the winds and seas were cooperative.

Chapter Seven

Adam and Martin arrived in Beaufort early Saturday. Martin went straight home to sleep so he'd be ready for a night out on the town. Adam, on the other hand, wasted no time telling his grandfather about the canal plans almost as soon as he'd made it up to the living quarters.

"This will change things, you know," said Emmanuel. "But it will be a long time before it happens, so don't get too excited. The changes may not even come in your lifetime, and certainly not in mine."

"Why not?" Adam asked, incredulous.

"Well, my boy, apart from this being an enormous undertaking that will cost a great deal of time and money, they've also left it to the civic-mindedness of local citizens to fund the effort."

"I wouldn't think that should be such a problem," said Adam.

"The men who give their money and put up labor to build the canal will make their investment back with the increased shipping traffic, wouldn't they?"

"How long do you think it will take to cut the canal?" Emmanuel asked.

Adam could tell his grandfather's question was a rhetorical one, but he answered it anyway.

"I don't know. A year or two?"

Emmanuel's eyes grew enormous and he let out a loud "Ha! Is that what you think?" He stood up from his favorite chair and went into the kitchen. "Oh to be young and so optimistic!"

Adam raised his eyebrows, then followed behind him. "What? What does that mean? How long do *you* think it will take?"

"Five years at a minimum," Emmanuel responded as he used a cloth to take the kettle from the fire and pour hot water into his cup and made tea. "And that's if everything goes off without a hitch. A decade or more is a likelier projection."

"Ten years? You mean because it will take so long for them to get started, right?"

"No. I mean because it's one thing to present a bill and have it signed into law, but the bill has no provision for the oversight of the assembly, and its dependence on a volunteer effort comes at a dreadful time." Emmanuel took his cup of tea and went back to his chair in the sitting room.

Adam knew he didn't need to ask why. His grandfather would tell him—probably more than he even wanted to know. He followed him again and sat on the settee beside Emmanuel's chair.

"What else have they recently signed into law there in New Bern? Hmm?"

Adam shook his head. "I don't know. All kinds of things. What do you mean?"

"Didn't we just talk about the fact that they just passed a substantial budget for Governor Tryon to build his palace in New Bern? Rest assured he'll spare no expense to have one of the finest homes in America! Never mind the number of taxpayers here is but a fraction of that of the more populous colonies."

"If you knew this project would take so long, why have you been so eager for it to be passed? I've heard you talk about how much we've needed this ever since I came here."

"Because I knew it would take so long, of course! I wanted at least to know there was some plan in place to see this come to fruition before the Lord calls me home."

"Don't say things like that!" said Adam. "You have right many years left, I'm sure. You may see that canal built before it's all over with."

Emmanuel shrugged. "Who knows? But I think it highly unlikely. Nevertheless, I still think there is cause for celebration."

Adam raised his eyebrows in surprise. "Alright. What'd you have in mind?"

"Since the weather's turned—I can tell because my joints are killing me—they'll no doubt have their annual hog killing over at Laney Martin's estate. I want you to go over there and talk to Cyrus and get us a pig. We'll dress it and put it on the pit Friday morning and have a barbecue on Friday. Put the word out that everyone's invited."

Adam nodded. "Will do."

Chapter Eight

AFTER A TYPICAL SUNDAY IN Beaufort, with church in the morning and rest all afternoon, Adam welcomed a regular workweek on Monday. They received some crates at the warehouse on a shipment from England. All day and night the warehouse was empty and otherwise quiet, except for the sounds of Adam's footsteps echoing up to the rafters as he crossed back and forth across the floor while counting and organizing the contents of a shipment.

Boaz worked through lunch, so by about four o'clock in the afternoon he was ready to quit for the day, but Adam had some inventory work to finish before he could stop for supper. Somehow he had ended up with a crate packed with what seemed to be every single variety of tiny item that had ever been received at Port Beaufort.

Both Boaz and Emmanuel had suggested he just stop for the day and come back to it in the morning. There was no rush, they told him. But Adam hated leaving a project undone. It would be on his mind all night, and he wouldn't be able to rest. No, when he set out to meet a goal, he intended to do, it and he wouldn't quit until he was finished.

It was close to nine o'clock when he finally counted the last of the patch boxes and was able to stop for the night. He was desperately curious to know if the crate beside it promised more of the same sort of contents, but he resisted the temptation to look inside. Even though taking inventory was a time-consuming process, when it involved crates filled to the brim with merchandise that had never before been seen by eyes in the American colonies, it could be as fascinating, just as at times as it could be tedious.

When Adam was first apprenticed at the shipping company the previous year, his curfew was eleven, but after he returned from Havana, Emmanuel told him he could stay out till midnight so long as he made it to work on time the next day. Most nights he was already knocked out and fast asleep before ten—after all, his day usually began at sunup—but this night he thought he'd take some extra time down at the tavern to unwind. Since it was understood that if any of the workers at his grandfather's warehouse worked especially late they were entitled to come in to work a little bit later the next morning, he knew it wouldn't be a problem.

From some distance away Adam could already hear the music coming out of the Topsail Tavern. It was a welcome sound. Valentine had gone for a couple of years without hiring regular musicians to play in his establishment, all thanks to a particularly nasty brawl that broke out one balmy spring night. During the summer, however, Mary finally convinced Valentine to bring in some decent regular musicians to play again, insisting that it would brighten her spirits while her son was traveling in the Caribbean. (Adam knew good and well that musicians playing in the tavern would have little effect on his mother's mood while he was away, but he also knew she was clever enough to use Valentine's concern for her own happiness to do something good for the tavern—something that Valentine was too stubborn to agree to for any other reason.)

It was change welcomed by everyone when Valentine finally started hiring some professional musicians to play on different nights of the week. The Topsail had its share of amateurs who would come in with fiddle, fife, or guitar in hand just to try and liven up the atmosphere—free of charge, of course—but the quality of that music was hit-or-miss, and more often than not left a lot to be desired.

The walk from the warehouse to the tavern chilled Adam to his bones. The weather had turned sharply cold in the past few days, and the wind coming off of the water seemed to drive the chill right through his layers of clothing.

When he opened the heavy door and stepped inside, he welcomed the warmth that filled the place from the great fireplace in the center of the dining room. There was Valentine, seated as always behind the bar, somehow simultaneously reading the paper while keeping an eye on the crowd for any customers in need of service or getting into mischief.

Three musicians—one with a guitar, one with a fiddle, and one with a tin whistle—were in the opposite corner of the establishment, performing a lively tune, while many of the patrons bobbed their heads from side to side and clapped their hands in time. Some of them even tried singing along, though few knew all the words. They didn't care. The patrons would just make something up and keep singing anyway.

It was Monday night, so Adam wasn't surprised that his mother had already gone to bed. While it was an unusually long workday for him, she had taken to turning in most nights before nine.

After giving a wave to Valentine, Adam found a seat at a small table near the kitchen, as the bar was full.

"What can I get for you?" asked Jackson.

The young server had moved up the ranks from being a busboy at the Topsail to a waiter the summer after Adam left for his apprenticeship.

"Hmm." Adam thought for a minute. "Tonight... tonight I think I'll have bumbo."

"Anything to eat?"

"Yeah... I haven't eaten yet. What did she make today?" Adam inquired.

He was, of course, referring to Aunt Franny, the old cook who'd been at the tavern since long before Adam was born and in fact was there even when his mother, Mary, first went to live there as a young girl.

"She made right many things," said Jackson, "but all that's left is fish stew, collards and fatback, and some sweet potatoes, I think. And corn fritters."

"Bring me some of all of it. I'm starving."

Jackson nodded and disappeared into the kitchen. While Adam waited on his food, he enjoyed listening to the music. It was nice to finally be able to just sit and take it in—a luxury he didn't have back in the days when he still lived and worked at the tavern. After another song the musicians took a break. The fellow with the tin whistle then started to play an old ballad, and things calmed down a bit.

Adam was taken by surprise when a man he did not know came up from behind him and said, "Mind if I sit here a bit, son?"

"Uh… no, sir… of course not. Have a seat." He motioned to the chair at the opposite side of the table.

The man, who looked to be in his forties, had black hair with silver strands running throughout. He sat down and appeared to look around for a server.

"If you're looking for the waiter, he'll be back here directly. He's got to bring me my supper."

The man smiled at Adam. "Your supper? It's awfully late to be eatin, ain't it?"

Adam tipped his head to the side and clicked his teeth. "Well, when you work late, what choice do you have?"

The man nodded. "True enough, I reckon."

Suddenly, it dawned on Adam that the man was the guitarist who had been playing that lively music just moments earlier.

"Oh, you're one of the musicians," he said.

The man nodded. "That I am, boy."

"You're new here. You play the guitar, right?"

"I do tonight, but sometimes I play the fiddle." The man's blue eyes twinkled as he talked about his talents. "Sometimes the flute. Sometimes even a little harpsichord."

"So you play all kinds of instruments? I can't even play one."

The man laughed. He extended his hand to shake Adam's. "I'm Benajah Hamilton. Friends call me Ben."

Adam shook his hand. "Pleased to make your acquaintance, Ben. I'm Adam Fletcher."

Ben looked around as if he was thinking of what to say next. Finally, he said, "You from around here? You come here often?"

Adam nodded. "Yep. This is my family's tavern. Valentine over there"—he tipped his head over in the direction of the bar—"is like my grandfather."

Ben turned around and looked over at Valentine, then looked back at Adam. "Hmph. I'd have never known."

Adam nodded. He really wasn't in the mood for small talk with a stranger. He was tired and didn't feel like doing the mental work that was necessary to carry on a conversation with someone who didn't have much to say, or a clear point to make.

"Hmm," said Ben. "So I reckon that confirms my suspicions."

Adam straightened his brow and glared at him but said nothing. His heart started to beat a little faster as he wondered if this man had any connection to Havana.

Ben could apparently see that Adam bristled at his comment. He seemed quick to speak up to clarify himself. "You must be Mary's son."

That wasn't helping. This man was on a first-name basis with his mother, or at least he thought he should be.

"I've spoken to her some." Ben was beginning to sound a little nervous at having to explain himself. "Well, obviously, since she works here every day. She's a right handsome woman, you know." He smiled at Adam. "You favor her, I'd say. Same hair, same eyes."

Adam made a genuine effort to relax his demeanor. He realized this man fancied his mother, and that was neither unusual nor alarming. Living in a port town, he'd seen that more times than he could count, though it was usually with salty sailors rather than multitalented musicians.

"That's kind of you," said Adam. "A lot of people say I look like my mother, but those who know my father say I look exactly like he did at my age."

Ben's face fell. "Your father?" He stammered, "Oh... I'm sorry. I didn't realize your mother was married... I mean, she didn't—"

Adam chuckled. "She didn't mention it? Well, I reckon she doesn't make a habit of discussing her personal life with strangers. You understand." He grinned.

"I sure do," said Ben.

Jackson brought Adam his mug of bumbo. "I'll get your supper out to you in just a minute." He turned and asked Ben, "Another beer?"

Ben nodded and waved over one of the other musicians.

"Toby, come on over here," he said.

The tall, red-haired man who had been playing the fiddle made his way across the dining room and turned a chair around backwards and sat straddling it. He held out his hand to shake Adam's.

"Tobias Cole. You can call me Toby."

Adam shook his hand. "Adam Fletcher. Nice to meet you."

Toby gave a little whistle to get Jackson's attention, then made a motion to him that he'd like a beer like Ben was having.

"Y'all sound real good," said Adam. "Been performing together long?"

"Together? Not too long," said Ben. "But long enough that we know how to read each other's cues."

Adam took a sip of his bumbo and gave a little nod. "I see."

"You got yourself some professional musicians here," said Toby. "We've probably got near about a hundred years of playing experience combined, but hardly any time playing together, and yet we sound like we've always been a trio, don't you think?"

Adam nodded. "I do. It's really lively, really adding some spice to this place."

Ben grinned. "That's what we do best, I reckon."

"My gracious," Adam remarked. "A hundred years' combined playing experience. Boy, that really sounds like something impressive when you put it like that."

Toby and Ben chuckled.

"That's the idea," said Toby. "It is true, though."

Ben nodded in agreement. "You got three of us, all in our forties, and we all been playing music since we were knee-high to a grasshopper, so there you have it—near 'bout a hundred years' experience."

Adam chuckled. "Very clever."

The three men sat sipping on their beverages. Adam felt a little awkward wondering what else they'd have to talk about. He hoped Jackson would come soon with his food.

Finally, he said, "So y'all aren't originally from around here, are you? At least I don't remember seeing y'all around until recently."

"Ah, well," said Ben, "I've been working my way down the coast from Maryland to get to my sister in South Carolina, playing music from place to place and taking on odd jobs to pay my way."

"James over there"—Toby motioned to the man playing the tin whistle—"and myself, we actually have been in this area before, years ago. We used to play over at Russell's, but we each went our separate ways for a time. When we met up again not too long ago, we tried to get work there again, but he said he already had plenty of musicians."

"So you heard Valentine was looking for somebody?" asked Adam.

"Mm-hmm," said Toby. "And it just worked out fine for all of us."

"Are y'all staying here at the tavern?" Adam asked.

Toby nodded. "Yep, for the time being, anyway. The three of us are sharing a room for now."

"Not for long, though," said Ben. "I don't reckon I'll be staying around here longer than it takes me to get enough money together to move on down the coast. Then James and Toby here will be able to spread out some in that room upstairs."

Adam nodded but really couldn't think of anything else to say.

There was another awkward silence. Then with seemingly perfect timing, Jackson showed up and delivered Adam's supper. After Adam bowed his head to quietly say grace, Toby and Ben both stood to excuse themselves.

"I reckon we'll let you enjoy your supper," said Toby. "It was nice to meet you."

"Nice to meet you fellas as well," said Adam.

"Hey, one thing," said Ben. "I'm always on the lookout for odd jobs. With you working so late and all, your boss might need an extra hand. Let me know if he's looking for anybody to take on—even temporarily."

Adam gave him a nod. "Will do."

Ben and Toby excused themselves and went back over to join James to play more music.

Of course Adam knew that Emmanuel wasn't one for hiring strangers, so it was unlikely he'd take on a traveling musician for even a temporary job at the warehouse.

Finally, much relieved, Adam would be able to enjoy his supper in quiet. He dug right in, and everything tasted so good to him. Nothing like exhaustion and hunger to make food taste even better. Just then Jackson sat down to visit with his former coworker and friend. The two chatted for a little while—or rather, Jackson did most of the talking—but Adam realized when he left the tavern that he must not've been paying close attention, because he couldn't remember most of what the boy had said.

He was so tired. He dreaded the long walk back to the warehouse. Just before he left, he asked Valentine if he was done with the paper that had arrived earlier that same day. Valentine said he was—at least the parts that interested him—and he gave it to him. Adam thanked him and asked him to say hello to his mother for him.

He bristled when he stepped out into the cold night from the warmth of the tavern. He buttoned up his overcoat and pulled the collar up around his ears, tucked the paper under his arm, and trudged back to the warehouse, the wind beating against his face the whole way.

He would sleep hard tonight.

Chapter Nine

As Adam walked back to the warehouse, he thought about the warm spell of the previous week, and he was grateful for it. He couldn't imagine taking Laney and Aunt Celie to New Bern in this weather, and certainly not by sail. He hoped a good time was being had by all in the Martin household, but not so fine a time as that Laney might choose to not come back to Beaufort.

When he finally made it back to the living quarters at the warehouse, he did his best to quietly tiptoe across the squeaky floor through the sitting room and into the kitchen, where he lit a short candle to take into his room.

He had to pass through Boaz's room first, but fortunately the middle-aged cooper was a deep sleeper, so Adam didn't have to worry about waking him as he passed through the room and into his own.

Adam had the newspaper tucked under his arm and the candle in his hand as he carefully turned the knob on the door handle and closed the door. He crossed the room and used the stubby candle to ignite the lantern that he kept on the nightstand, and he placed the newspaper there next to it. He removed his hat, coat, and waistcoat, then sat on the edge of his bed and pulled off his shoes before turning down the blankets and crawling under the covers. He loosed the cord that had been holding his dark hair out of his face and closed his eyes as he massaged the back of his neck and head where it had gotten sore from craning forward counting odds and ends all day. He also really hated wearing his hair back—it gave him headaches—but it was more practical when he was working to keep the hair out his face.

Once he'd eased the pain a bit, he took the *Gazette* in hand. He'd been looking forward to reading that paper ever since he'd seen it at the tavern. Knowing he'd just been in James Davis's print shop several days earlier, where this very paper was being printed, fascinated him.

He skipped quickly past the front page. It rarely featured anything of local interest. Instead, the front page was usually occupied either with official public notices of new laws, or else long serials that would run in several issues – things like "The Life and Times of Marcus Antonius", or an essay on the political and civil rights of British colonists. More often than not, regional news items were relegated to the last page.

Sprinkled among the local items were advertisements from local merchants, real estate listings, and legal notices. There was one item from a poor man called Nicholas Sims that read, "Whereas my wife Henrietta Sims has left my bed and board; I forewarn all persons from trusting her on my account, as I will pay no debt of her contracting."

Adam shook his head. *Poor fella*, he thought. *It's bad enough his wife has run out on him, but to have to put it in the paper...*

As he scanned through the advertisements to see if there was anything else that looked interesting, a news item caught his eye. Mr. Davis did not typically use larger letters above local news items. He seemed to reserve those for notices and advertisements. But in spite of the words not being any bigger on the page than any other, they still jumped out at Adam: "highwaymen," "knocked in the head," and "murder." This news item was accompanied by its own notice at the bottom of its column, as though it had likely been inserted at the last minute. It was a warning that said, "It is believed these two violent criminals were heading north and are possibly on their way to Williamsburg; however, it is also possible that they are in the vicinity of New Bern or Swift Creek, and the greatest caution should be exercised in apprehending them, as they are armed and dangerous. Any person with information leading to their capture will receive a reward. TEN POUNDS."

This is that attack we heard about in New Bern. The attack had happened about a week earlier. Adam figured whoever these highwaymen were, it was unlikely that they would have stayed around New Bern. They were probably long gone by now. Furthermore, they could have ultimately gone in any direction. Adam couldn't imagine why the paper would have said that they were possibly on their way to Williamsburg. How could anyone know where they were headed if no one even knew who they were?

To make matters more difficult, the surviving victim wasn't even found until late in the day—several hours after they were attacked. Mr. Davis had not been informed of all of the details, or at the very least, if he had he had chosen not to print them in his paper. But from what Adam had learned from Will, the story went like this:

A woman and her husband were traveling home in their horse cart after visiting relatives in the territory between Handcock and Slocomb Creeks. The first night of the journey, they made camp about seven miles south of New Bern. Shortly before daybreak the two highwaymen descended upon their camp. One of the men demanded that they hand over all of their valuables and planned to steal their horse, but the other man didn't think that was enough and decided he wanted a go at the woman as well.

He urged his partner to restrain the husband while he had his turn at the wife. The husband lunged at the man and attacked him for making the suggestion, at which point the would-be rapist knocked him in side of the head with the butt of his pistol, causing him to fall immediately unconscious.

The other highwayman balked at the idea and said he didn't mind stealing but wouldn't go along with assaulting the poor woman, who was apparently crouched down on her knees in fear at the feet of the man who intended to rape her. He held her in place by the hair of her head so that she could not get away.

The men argued, and apparently the more compassionate one convinced the other that, with the sun coming up, they should hurry and take what they need and be on their way. They attempted to take the horse, but she reared up in defiance and ran away into the surrounding marsh as soon as she was untied. The two men, frustrated by their failed efforts to secure a speedy escape, then took off running in a northerly direction.

The woman tried unsuccessfully to revive her husband, so she decided to go in search of help on foot. She walked for a couple of hours but ultimately was overcome with worry and exhaustion and began to feel confused about where she was going, so she sat down to rest and fell asleep.

Thankfully, the horse that escaped made its way to a farm a few miles away, nearer to New Bern. The owner of the farm recognized the very distinctive white markings on the black horse and knew the family to whom it belonged. Considering the horse had come from the road to the south, he smartly thought to take one of his slaves and his own horse cart and head down that road in case there was someone in trouble. He found the woman a few miles down the road and she led him to the camp, where her husband still lay motionless.

Sadly, by the time they arrived the man's body was stiff. He must have suffered a bleed in his brain from the blow to his temple and died.

The farmer and his slave loaded the man's body into the cart and took it and the woman back to their estate on the south side of the Neuse River. The constable in that territory was able to get some local men together to search for clues near the camp but found nothing remarkable and therefore had little to go on beyond the woman's testimony.

At this point the only way the local authorities could hope to make a break in the case would be if a good citizen came forward with information. And of course that wouldn't likely happen without the promise of a financial reward.

Adam shook his head in disbelief as he recalled the details he had heard about the crime. He hadn't given it much thought since they had talked about it that night around the supper table, but seeing it in the paper reminded him of it. He couldn't help but think about Laney, and even Will's wife, Catherine, being at risk of such an attack if the two men were hanging around New Bern.

Since no physical descriptions had been provided in the paper, there wasn't much to go on in terms of identifying the culprits. Apparently, because of the poor lighting at the time of the attack the female victim was unable to describe the men other than to say that one was a bit taller than the other, but both were of average weight and height. She couldn't see their hair, since the taller one was wearing a dark-colored Monmouth cap, and the shorter man wore a tricorn. She also said that she couldn't guess how old they were, but she thought they were older than her. She was only twenty-two, though, so that wasn't especially helpful.

He tried to push the thoughts out of his mind about Laney being at risk with those men at large. He knew there was little likelihood of anything happening to her while she was there visiting with her brother and sister-in-law. He also knew that with his experiences of the last year, he tended to feel heightened anxiety about any potentially risky situation. Emmanuel had warned him to be ever vigilant in life but to not succumb to looking for a devil behind every bush. He determined there was no cause for concern without a clear reason to believe the men were in New Bern, and that with any luck they were either already apprehended and in custody, or far beyond the borders of the colony.

At that he continued reading through the paper's other announcements, then finally blew out his lantern and went to sleep.

Chapter Ten

"THANK THE LORD," ADAM EXCLAIMED.

He was relieved that the crates he had to inventory today were not filled with as many small items as the ones from yesterday. One of today's crates held blankets and small rugs, while the other contained an assortment of hats for men and women.

Poor Martin, on the other hand, was stuck inventorying a crate of sewing supplies, including buttons and thimbles—many of which had spilled out of the boxes that were meant to keep them sorted.

"Serves you right," said Adam. "You wouldn't help me yesterday. You were mocking me for having to go through all of those ladies' knickknacks. Looks like you're reaping what you've sown."

Martin rolled his eyes at Adam. "Oh, be quiet." He squinted

his eyes and went back to sorting thimbles and putting them back into their little boxes.

Each box was meant to hold a certain number of a particular design. Martin had to pick up each thimble and look at the markings on the side and separate them into their own little piles. Then he had to count them out into the specified number for each box set.

"Headache, Martin?"

He didn't need to ask. Adam already knew his friend was struggling thanks to another hard night of drinking.

Martin didn't respond. He just gave Adam an annoyed look and went back to sorting thimbles.

"You keep on drinking like you been doing lately, you're gonna end up dead in a ditch."

Boaz sat quietly making inventory of a group of small crates of iron cookware, but he couldn't help but say something when he heard that.

"I think the boy's got a point there, Smith. You trying to pickle yourself or somethin?"

"I have no idea what y'all are talking about. I'm just tired. I didn't sleep worth nothin last night—froze my tail off."

"What's the problem? You out of firewood?" Adam jokingly asked.

"Maybe he just couldn't find a woman to keep him warm," suggested Boaz.

The two of them laughed, and Martin nodded and feigned amusement as they joked at his expense.

Finally, Adam said, "Didn't you say you were going over to Jones's house last night to play cards with him and Canady?"

Martin nodded unexpressively. "Yep."

"Oh," said Adam. "You lost your purse, didn't you?"

"You've got to learn to quit when you're ahead, Smith," said Boaz.

Adam shook his head. "I hate it for you, Martin. I really do. Seems like things have just been downhill for you lately."

"You're damned right," said Martin. "Ever since we got to Cuba, in fact, it's like the Fates are conspiring against me."

Just then Emmanuel slowly and stiffly made his way across the warehouse to speak to his workers. "What's all this Fates nonsense, Smith?"

Martin exchanged a sheepish grin with Adam and Boaz. Adam imagined Martin must've been thinking that it was bad luck that Emmanuel had come in when he did. Everyone knew he didn't have much patience for superstitions, or what he called "pagan colloquialisms," like talking about bad luck or the Fates, a frequent source of joking behind Emmanuel's back, since sailors were among the most superstitious of all men, and his industry was full of them.

They were all thankful when Emmanuel quickly changed the subject rather than going into a speech about Fate versus Providence.

"I just got done talking to Faulkner Baldwin." He had his hand on his back, rubbing it as if it was hurting him terribly. "We're having a citizen's meeting on Friday to discuss the business of the new canal. Adam will be going to get a pig tomorrow morning, and I want you boys to be ready to butcher and roast it so we can enjoy a nice barbecue after the meeting."

"We're having a party?" asked Martin with a mischievous grin.

Emmanuel sighed and gave a curt nod. "A barbecue, Mr. Smith, not a bacchanalia. I'll be inviting all of the gentlemen who attend the meeting, as well as their families. This'll be no time for you to lose your inhibitions. Furthermore, this cold weather has angered my old bones, and it certainly doesn't help my patience levels, so don't push me."

"Don't worry, Emmanuel," said Boaz. "We'll keep him in line." He looked at Adam and grinned. "Right, Fletcher?"

"I'm sure he'll behave himself," Adam agreed.

"Hmm…" Emmanuel seemed like he wanted to say something but stopped short.

After a second or two he said, "I should tell you, Smith, if you come to work in this condition again I'll relieve you of your employment until you can see fit to dry yourself out." He started to hobble back towards the stairs, then turned back to say one more thing. "And you tell Jones I said the same thing if he's in a state as bad as you."

Martin nodded and gave an embarrassed half smile. "Yes, sir."

Adam and Boaz tried hard not to even smile, but Adam, at least, was laughing on the inside.

Emmanuel slowly climbed the stairs to the living quarters.

"You know, Fletcher, it's a good thing Emmanuel don't let you come with us to play cards," said Martin. "We're real bad influences."

Adam could tell Martin was being facetious, so he rolled his eyes at him.

"Of course Emmanuel don't want him hangin around with you over at Jones's place," said Boaz. "He wants better for his grandson than to turn out like either of you rascals."

"Emmanuel's been a rascal in his day, and I reckon he's turned out alright," Martin countered.

"That was different," said Adam. "He was running around with pirates, after all. I'd say a little bit of wild living goes with the territory, doesn't it? You and Jones, on the other hand, y'all just like to drown yourselves in the bottle. And you've gotten far worse since we've gotten back from Havana."

"I have not," said Martin.

"You have! You absolutely have. Now I can see why Emmanuel probably never sent you and Jones out on the same voyages before. He knew y'all would bring out the worst in each other."

"Ain't that the truth?" Boaz agreed.

Adam felt a little guilty for giving his friend a hard time, but the truth was Martin *had* seemed to be going downhill ever since they returned from Havana. Something had changed him. He seemed intent on engaging in increasingly self-destructive behaviors. He'd liked to have a good time and drink a little more than the next fellow for as long as Adam had known him, but now it was almost as if his goal was to stay drunk as much as possible and practice whatever vices he could conjure up at every available opportunity. He'd disappear for days at a time and no one knew where he'd gone, then turn up again for work like nothing had happened.

The truth was Adam worried about where it would lead. In all his years growing up at the tavern, he'd seen many men take a destructive turn—to the point where Valentine had to ban some from the establishment. Never had any of those fellows gotten their acts together without some major tragedy happening to them first. Some never did get their acts together but ended up dead in a ditch—like Adam had warned Martin earlier—or something similar.

Thing was, Adam didn't think Martin's worsening behavior could be entirely attributed to the influence of hanging around Ricky Jones, although that certainly exacerbated the situation.

No. Adam felt certain something else was causing Martin to act this way, but it was anyone's guess what it could be.

Chapter Eleven

FIRST THING THURSDAY MORNING, ADAM took Emmanuel's horse cart and headed over to the Martin estate to buy a pig for the barbecue. As he made the trip in the bitter cold, he amused himself thinking back on the livestock that he saw roaming through the streets in New Bern. He had heard stories about Beaufort from some of the old folks, who remembered when hogs used to run wild in the town. They actually had to pass a law that said any hogs found running loose could be killed on the spot, with half of the hog going to the person who rid the town of the porcine nuisance, and the other half going to the church for the benefit of the parish.

Barbecuing a pig had been a social staple of the coastal region of the colony for as long as anybody could remember. There sure were plenty of pigs to go around, and the meat could feed nearly everyone in a small town.

Adam did neglect to mention one thing to Emmanuel: while he knew all about eating barbecue, he knew next to nothing about buying a pig, transporting one, butchering one, *or* roasting one. Back at the tavern, barbecue was not on the menu, so there was no cause for Adam to have ever learned.

That's alright, he thought. *I'm sure Cyrus will help me figure out what I'll need. How hard can it be to buy a pig?*

When he arrived at the estate, he was surprised to find Will's carriage there. Though he had planned to go straight to the servant's cabin to talk to Cyrus, he instead went around to the riverfront side of the house and up on the porch to knock on the door.

Laney answered it. "Oh, Adam! Good morning!"

Adam's brown eyes grew large and his jaw dropped. "What are y'all doing back?" He stood there shivering.

"Come in," Laney insisted, motioning for him to come inside. "It's freezing out here."

Adam smiled and stepped into the house. "Thank you. It was a cold ride over here." He looked around to see if anyone else was there. "When did you get here?"

"We got in yesterday evening. There's been another attack, and they think it might be one or both of the men responsible for attacking that couple last week."

"Another attack? Was it a murder?"

Laney shook her head. "No, thank the Lord, though I wouldn't be surprised if the girl didn't wish she was dead."

Adam's eyes grew large at that statement. He knew that must mean it was a particularly bad situation.

"A young woman named Penelope Wilson was brutally

attacked Monday night," Laney explained. "Then she was left injured and shivering just down the road from the estate where she's bound in service as a servant."

"What in the world!" Adam exclaimed. "And they think it's the same men who did it?"

"Mm-hmm—well, one of them, anyway. Of course it hasn't been in the papers yet, but my brother took us out of New Bern just as soon as he heard about it. Obviously, he doesn't want Catherine and their child at risk, or me, with violent men on the loose."

"Good Lord!" Adam was deeply concerned but relieved that Will hadn't wasted time and brought them back to Beaufort right away, though the thought didn't escape him that danger could have fallen upon them on the road south of the Trent, as that was where the first incident had taken place. "How'd your brother find out about it?" he asked.

"Down at the courthouse early Tuesday morning."

"So all of you came in your brother's carriage?" asked Adam.

Laney shook her head. "No, Aunt Celie didn't want to come back with us, since her son would be in New Bern. She wanted to stay there and look after him, I suppose, though I don't know what she thinks she can do for him at her age."

"I don't know"—Adam chuckled—"I'm guessing she might be a swift hand with a frying pan."

Laney smiled. "True." After a couple of seconds she wrinkled her brow and said, "Wait, what are *you* doing here?"

"Oh well, Emmanuel sent me to buy a pig from Cyrus. They're having a citizen's meeting here in town on Friday morning, and he wants to have a barbecue that afternoon and invite everyone."

"What's the meeting about?"

"The canal. I told him what I'd heard in New Bern, about

them passing that law about the canal. He says it's been a long time coming, and it'll be a long time yet before it ever happens, but he wanted to get 'civic-minded gentlemen' together to discuss possible plans and everyone's intentions for how they will be contributing to the effort."

"I see. Well, won't you come sit down and have some breakfast?" Laney offered. "I can't promise it'll be as good as Aunt Celie's cooking, but I suppose it's hard to go wrong with hot grits and bacon, isn't it?"

Adam grinned. "I reckon it is."

He followed Laney into the dining room and half expected to see Catherine or Will sitting there, but the room was empty. *Does this mean the two of us are completely alone?* Adam smiled as he wondered.

"Have a seat," said Laney, motioning to the chair at the head of the table. Then she disappeared into the kitchen.

Adam hesitated, then sat down. He still had his hat under his arm and looked around for where he could put it. He ended up quickly peeking under the table and deciding to stick his hat in the empty chair next to him. As he observed the room, Adam noticed the paintings on the wall above the room's grand fireplace. One was of a man with medium-brown hair and piercing blue eyes. The other was a woman with blond hair—lighter than Laney's—and striking green eyes. They had to be Laney's mother and father. They were both very attractive people.

Martin wasn't joking when he said good looks ran in the family. Both Laney and Will, as well as their roguish cousin, were all… well… *stunning.* Their looks couldn't be more different than those of Adam and his parents, who had dark features.

On the adjacent interior wall there hung three more portraits, easily identifiable by the very large, very fancy powdered wigs as being from the early part of the century. Two of the portraits were of men, one was of a woman. Adam guessed they were likely to be the grandparents, although one of the grandmothers was obviously missing from the group. His mind wandered as he contemplated the many reasons why she might never have sat for a portrait, or why at the very least there wasn't one of her displayed.

Laney soon returned carrying a breakfast tray. She appeared a little unsteady—or maybe even nervous—as she brought it over and sat it down on the table near where Adam was seated. She placed in front of him a bowl of very stiff-looking grits and a plate with several thick pieces of bacon, which without question were overcooked.

"Oh... my goodness!" said Adam. He was trying very hard to look enthusiastic about the meal, but without laughing. "You did cook grits and bacon. How about that?"

Laney gave him a half smile. "Well, remember I said it won't be as good as Aunt Celie makes it, but it's cooked all the way anyhow."

Adam raised his eyebrows. "Yes, I see that it is! Well done. Very well done, Miss Laney."

He looked down and noticed he didn't have any silverware yet. "You don't happen to have a spoon, do you?"

Laney glanced down and saw the silverware and linen napkin were still on the tray. "Oh gracious, yes."

She quickly placed them in front of him and then gave a little nod as if to say, *Go ahead. Try it.*

Adam looked at her and grinned. *Oh Lord, she is beautiful,* he thought, *but I don't have the foggiest idea what this is going to taste like. Just help me not to hurt her feelings.*

He picked up a piece of bacon and took a bite. "Mmm… crispy!"

Her eyes were anxiously fixed on him to see if he'd say anything else.

"It's good!" he added.

He picked up his spoon and looked down at his bowl of grits, which formed very stiff peaks, and he wondered if they'd be edible. Grits didn't usually hold a shape like that.

"Laney," he said, "I hope you don't mind me asking, but I got awfully thirsty on the way over here. Do you happen to have anything I can wash this down with?"

Her eyes grew large in embarrassment. "Oh! I completely forgot! Would you like tea, or cider, or water, or coffee?"

"Hmm… cider would be good." *Can't go wrong with cider*, he thought.

She gave him a quick nod and scurried back into the kitchen.

Adam tentatively took a taste of the grits and realized they had no salt. He contemplated whether he should ask her for any salt, or whether he should just break up his bacon into the bowl like he'd normally do with grits and hope that seasoned them enough. He decided that would probably be the most gracious way to handle it.

When Laney returned with a mug of cider, Adam was crumbling his bacon up into the grits and stirring them around.

"I do that too!" she remarked.

"It's the only way to eat grits, I say," said Adam.

He loaded his spoon with a great mound of the stuff and quickly popped it into his mouth. *This is terrible*, he thought.

"Oh, I meant to ask you if you'd like any salt or butter," said Laney.

Adam chewed up the mouthful of grits and bacon—which

took longer than he would've liked, so that the bacon seemed to grow in his mouth—and he swallowed it, then said, "Oh well, sure. If you have any. I might have a little bit."

Laney went back into the kitchen and came out with a salt dish and the butter crock.

As Adam dressed up the grits with the seasonings, he motioned for Laney to sit down, but she only raised her eyebrows. It occurred to Adam that he ought to get up and pull out a chair for her, so he did. Turned out he pulled out the chair that had his hat in it. He looked down and saw it, and just as she was about to take a seat he reached over into the chair and pulled his hat away. He knew she had to be wondering what he was doing.

He showed her the hat in his hand and then moved it to the other chair. She sat down, as did he, and they just sat and smiled at each other for a moment. Adam was thinking it must have also occurred to her that this was their first time being completely alone.

Finally, Laney spoke up and asked, "Well? Do you like it?"

It took Adam a second to answer. "Oh... yes! It's very good." He started eating again. "Very good. I guess your brother and his wife have already eaten."

Laney tipped her head to the side in disappointment. "Well, they came down and had tea, but neither of them were very hungry yet, so they've gone for a walk on the grounds."

"They have?" Adam asked as he started to eat another spoonful of grits. He was thankful they at least were seasoned a little bit now, even if they were dry and overcooked. "But it's so cold outside," he said. "Why in the world would they want to go for a walk now?"

"I know. I said the same thing, but Catherine just reminded me that she's only ever been here once before, and she really didn't remember the place very well. She wanted to see the improvements we've done over the last couple of years since her last visit."

Adam reckoned they might have sneaked off to eat something else.

With seemingly perfect timing, Will and Catherine returned to the house and came into the dining room.

"Adam!" Will exclaimed, crossing the room to greet him. "What brings you out here this morning?"

Adam stood from his chair to shake hands with Will. "Good morning, Will, Catherine."

"Good morning, Adam. It's nice to see you again so soon," said Catherine.

Adam sat back down to finish eating. "Well, Emmanuel sent me over here to buy a pig. We're having a barbecue tomorrow after the citizen's meeting about the new canal. Laney here invited me in to have something to eat before I went to talk to Cyrus, though."

Will looked at Adam's bowl and then raised his eyebrows at Adam. "Oh, you're sampling my sister's culinary skills, are you?"

A very small smile could be seen at the corners of Adam's mouth, but he fought it hard so that it wouldn't turn into a ridiculous grin or fit of laughter.

"I sure am. She clearly has many undiscovered talents," said Adam.

Laney blushed and smiled, then looked at her brother as if to say, *See, he doesn't think my cooking is awful!*

"Well, when you're done eating there," said Will, "you come on outside, and we'll have Cyrus help you select a pig."

"Won't you sit down and join me?" Adam asked Will and his wife. "Laney said you hadn't eaten yet. I guess your walk has helped you build up an appetite."

Will looked at Laney. He then turned and looked at his wife. Catherine made a face that indicated to Adam that this whole situation was very awkward.

Will ended up responding, "We really weren't that hungry, but you know, it's a funny thing—when we were outside having our walk just now, Cyrus called to us from his cabin and told us that his wife was so happy to see we had arrived last night that she made a molasses cake and wanted to give us some."

"Hmph." Adam smiled as he continued eating the stiff grits and overcooked bacon. "I see." He pointed at the bowl with his spoon as he said with a mouthful, "Well, you are really missing something good here."

"Oh, I don't doubt it," said Will.

Catherine nodded in agreement.

"But what could we do?" Will continued. "We barely even know Cyrus's wife. They only married a short time ago. We could hardly say no to her."

Adam nodded. "I understand." He grinned as he finished the last spoonful of grits and bacon in the bowl and then said to Laney, "That was delicious. I would love to sample anything you decide to make."

Laney smiled and took a deep breath in what looked very much like exhilaration.

"Now," said Adam, "let's go get that pig."

Chapter Twelve

Laney and Catherine opted to stay behind while Will took Adam out to see a man about a pig.

"Cyrus," Will called out as he led Adam across the lawn to Cyrus's cabin. "Our friend Adam Fletcher has some business to talk with you."

A young man in his twenties with a copper-brown complexion and closely cropped hair came over to greet them. Adam wasn't sure what he had been doing, but apparently it had gotten his hands dirty, because he was wiping them on a rag as he came over to speak to them.

"Yes, sir. What can I do for ya?" asked Cyrus.

Just then Catherine called to Will from the house. Before Adam had a chance to answer Cyrus, Will said, "I'll leave you to it, men. Cyrus, give him the family price, please."

He turned and started walking briskly back towards the house.

"Happy to," Cyrus called after him. Then he turned to Adam and said, "But I need to know what I'm giving you the family price for."

Adam chuckled. "I reckon you do. Well, Emmanuel Rogers sent me over here to buy a pig. We're having a barbecue tomorrow."

Cyrus nodded and smiled as if he liked the sound of that. "Alright! Alright, come on then."

He started walking towards the barn and pig pen. Adam followed.

"Just come on over here and see which one looks like it'll suit you. I'll tell you if it's a good one."

Cyrus's wife came around that same time—presumably to feed scraps to the pigs—but Adam guessed it was really to see who he was.

"What y'all doin?" said the diminutive young woman with a chipper, youthful voice.

She was heavily pregnant and wore a lavender-colored dress and had her head wrapped in a cloth like a turban—like Aunt Celie often wore.

"This here is Mr. Adam Fletcher. Emmanuel Rogers done sent him over to fetch a pig 'fore we do our hog killin. Mr. Adam, this is my wife, Violet."

Adam smiled at her. "Pleased to meet you."

"And you, sir," she said with a little curtsey.

Adam leaned over the fence and said, "Yep. I'm trying to decide on one right now."

He studied over the pigs in the pen—nearly all of which had different patterns of black and white spots—but he didn't have the foggiest idea about how to choose one, so he decided to pick the one that looked best to him.

"How about that one over there?" he said, pointing to a healthy-looking pig that seemed particularly energetic.

Adam could hear Violet laugh. She didn't even try to be subtle about it. Adam raised his eyebrows in confusion and looked over at Cyrus, unsure of what she meant.

Cyrus did a much better job of maintaining a straight face. "No. No, I don't think you want that one, Mr. Adam."

"Really? Why not?" said Adam. "It looks healthy to me."

"Oh she's healthy alright," said Violet. She snickered, then waved her hand dismissively at them and started walking towards an outdoor area where there was a giant tub positioned over a raised pile of wood. "You tell him, Cyrus. Ain't gon' do him no good if you don't teach him nothin. I reckon I'll go get the scaldin tub ready."

Adam noticed she was starting a fire under the tub. Cyrus stepped over and stood right next to Adam. "Well, ah, sir, that sow is in season."

Adam was thoroughly confused now. "In season?"

"Ya see, ah well, she tryin to attract a boar hog—to make li'l pigs—but they ain't any boar hogs out here right now. See, we take care of most of the boar hogs when they little." He made a snipping motion with his fingers. "You understand?"

Adam's eyes grew large and he clenched his teeth in mild horror, considering the sad circumstances of those male pigs. "Oh, I see."

He gave Cyrus a confused look. He then looked over at the sow. "But wait, how can you tell that sow is in season?"

Cyrus looked like he was trying to decide whether he should explain. Apparently, he decided against it.

"Just you trust me," he said. "When you 'round pigs and you raisin 'em, it's your business to know when they tryin' to do their business. We got a boar hog, but we don't keep him here in the same pen with the sows. All the male pigs in this pen done been fixed." Cyrus lowered his eyes at Adam. "You understand, sir?"

Adam did understand. What he didn't understand, however, was how Cyrus could possibly tell that sow was *in season*. He sure couldn't tell standing where he was just by looking at her. Second, he didn't know what in the world that had to do with slaughtering her for barbecue anyway.

Adam chuckled. "I'll take your word on it," he said. He studied the animals in the pen again but decided it was probably a waste of his time, as well as Cyrus's, for him to try to choose a pig. "Why don't you just pick out a good one for me?" he said.

Cyrus looked like he was thinking about it for a moment. Then he nodded at Adam. "Alright. I'll do it. I reckon I ought to be able to find you just what you're lookin for. How big you want it?"

"Emmanuel said about seventy-five pounds dressed weight."

Cyrus nodded, then walked down the length of the fence. "Seventy-five pounds." He looked over the different pigs and said, "I think any of these three over here ought to be fine for what you needin."

Adam saw the animals he was pointing at. "Yeah, I'd say any of those look fine. How about that one there?" The pig he'd chosen had a mostly black body, but its sides, hindquarters, and legs were mottled with white. It also had a whitish pattern on its face around its snout.

"Alright then," said Cyrus. "I'll get this one ready for you. Violet's got to get that scaldin tub heated first, though."

"What does that do?" Adam asked.

"After we kill the pig, we got to get all that hair off 'fore we can start to butcher him."

Adam looked again at the pig they had chosen. "How will you kill him?"

"Oh, I'll hit him in the noggin with a hammer." Cyrus tapped on his own head where his hairline met his forehead. "One good hit ought to knock him right out, then I'll stick him," he motioned to his neck, "right here. Drain out all his blood. Then we can put him in the scaldin tub."

Sounded like messy business—far messier than killing chickens, something to which Adam was actually quite accustomed. One only had to wring their necks before cleaning and butchering them.

Adam was still wondering about what Cyrus had told him earlier. He had to know. "Why is it bad to eat a pig *in season?*"

Adam made a face as he asked a question. The idea sounded off-putting in and of itself, but he wondered if there was some other reason why it was a bad thing to do.

Cyrus looked at Adam and said, "You really want me to tell you?"

Adam chuckled, then said, "Well, maybe not."

Cyrus quickly walked over to the barn and grabbed a hammer, some rope, and a knife, then came back over to Adam and said, "When a sow's in season, it sure 'nuff won't kill ya, but it'll give meat that's tainted—smells real strong, and then it won't taste as good. You know if somethin don't smell right, ain't nobody gon' wanna eat it."

Adam nodded in agreement.

"Listen, sir," said Cyrus. "It's gon' take me a few hours to get the hog ready for you. If you want to, you can go take care of some other things while we doin this here. I reckon I'll have him ready for you to pick up by three."

"That's fine with me," said Adam.

He thanked Cyrus and left him to do his job. He would've liked to stay and watch, just to see how the process worked, but he got the impression Cyrus would rather he go on inside.

Adam decided to return to the warehouse to help Boaz with getting the barbecue pit ready. He would come back later in the afternoon to get the pig.

Chapter Thirteen

IT WAS STILL DARK OUT, and Adam desperately wanted to sleep, but Boaz stood at his door telling him it was time to get up.

"Rise and shine, Fletcher. The fire's good and hot. Get on up so you can come help me cook this thing."

"Ahhgghh." Adam groaned as he forced himself to turn over, which wasn't easy considering he was buried under the weight of three heavy quilts to keep warm. The room was always so cold in the morning, and there was something about being woken up when it was still dark that made it feel even colder.

He liked having a window looking out on Taylor Creek next to his bed, but this time of year, in spite of the heavy curtain he'd hang over it at night, there was still a terrible draft that would come in over the framework.

Boaz hadn't moved from the doorway, and Adam could sense he was still there, even though his eyes weren't open yet.

"Bo, are you going to keep standing there?"

"When I know you're awake, I'll leave."

"Fine." Adam growled into his pillow. He turned his head to look at Boaz and opened his eyes. "I'm awake." He propped himself up on his elbows, then dropped his feet off of the side of the bed and pulled the quilts around him.

Boaz stood there for another few seconds, then turned to go back through his room and into the kitchen. As he walked away, he called back to Adam, "Don't lay back down. You'll fall asleep again. Get on up and get movin."

Adam knew as much as he wanted to crawl back into bed, he really did need to get up. Actually, he was looking forward to learning how to cook a pig—a whole pig, not just the cuts of meat Aunt Franny would fix for the tavern.

It would be noon or even later before the pig was done. Emmanuel's plan was to wrap up the meeting no later than eleven, then tell everyone to go home, bring their families, and enjoy a pig pickin that afternoon.

After he got dressed and went downstairs, he had to help Boaz lift the split pig over the fire. It had been made in a pit in the ground not too far from the warehouse.

Several hours later—by the time the meeting was over and folks would start coming to enjoy the fruits of their smoky labor—Adam felt like an expert at cooking pigs. He watched as Boaz demonstrated for him how to cut away large portions of a cooked pig and begin chopping it up.

"You don't want to chop it up too much," he warned. "Just enough to break it up some and get the meat mixed up good with the crispy skin." He quickly pulled some more aside and chopped it before popping a strip in his mouth. "Mmm-mmm! Go on, pull you a piece."

Adam reached down and tried to grab a piece that looked like it still had a bit of skin attached. He nearly burnt his fingers, but he didn't care. He couldn't wait to eat. He knew it would be delicious.

He understood exactly what Boaz meant about how to chop the meat—and they wouldn't really chop it all. They'd leave much of it intact on the pig so that folks could come along and "pick" it, hence the term "pig pickin."

While the pig was cooking, Boaz had shown Adam how to make the vinegar sauce that would douse the pork when it was served. It had been seasoned throughout the cooking process, but this would be a final step of flavoring.

Meanwhile, Aunt Franny was cooking collards, stewed potatoes, and fried cornbread, along with some pies that would be delivered from the Topsail Tavern.

Adam was surprised when Valentine came to bring the food and saw his mother had come along. He hadn't expected her to be there. He went over to meet them. Valentine and Mary climbed out and walked around to the back of the cart to start unloading the food.

"Y'all want some music over here today?" said Valentine.

"How's that?" Adam asked as he grabbed one of the large pots of vegetables and led Valentine and his mother towards the warehouse, where they would set everything up.

"It was his idea," said Mary, motioning her head back towards Valentine as she grabbed a huge basket full of cornbread from the horse cart. She followed behind them into the warehouse and carried the basket over to the area where the food would be served and put it on top of a long table that had been fashioned out of several tall barrels and long boards. "Last night Valentine told those boys who've been playing together at the tavern about the pig pickin and mentioned they could come over here and entertain, maybe make a little extra money. You think Emmanuel would like that? If he'll hire 'em, Valentine can let 'em know as soon as he gets back over there."

Adam smiled. "I think that's a fine idea. They'll liven things up."

Valentine nodded. "I sure think so. All the big parties have some kind of music, but I figured ol' Emmanuel might not remember that, since it's probably been so long since he had one."

"You're probably right," said Adam. "I'll mention it to Boaz, and then he can find out."

Just then Boaz came into the warehouse.

"Speak of the devil," said Adam. "Hey, Bo. Valentine suggested we hire the musicians from over at the tavern to play for the pig pickin. You think Emmanuel would agree to that?"

Boaz raised his eyebrows in surprise. "I don't see why not. That'd be good. Who are they?"

"They're a trio," said Mary. "One plays the fiddle, one plays guitar, and one plays a flute... No... what's that thing called? A tin whistle."

"I think they're good, and they must be willing to work cheap if Valentine's hired 'em," Adam joked.

Boaz chuckled. "I can't see Emmanuel findin any fault with that. Tell 'em to come on down."

"Will do," said Valentine. "In fact, I've got to get on back to the tavern now."

When he left the warehouse, Adam and Mary followed him out.

Valentine climbed back up into the driver's seat of the horse cart. "Some of us gotta work."

Mary started to get back into the cart as well, but Valentine said to her, "No, no, missy! Why don't you just stay here and enjoy the party? You're not workin today."

Mary shook her head at Valentine, then looked at Adam defensively and said, "I'm not working in the tavern today, but I've got washing to do."

Adam wrinkled his brow. "But it's already lunchtime. And it's cold out. By the time you get home and get the washing done, the sun'll be going down. Then what are you gonna do? Hang out the washing in the dark?"

"The boy's right," said Valentine. "Stay here. You need to get out of the tavern—be around some regular folks. You don't even have the Widow Simpson to go see anymore. You're turning into a hermit."

Mary sighed. She apparently couldn't think of another excuse to leave, and neither Adam nor Valentine would help her come up with one.

"Come on, Mama," said Adam. "Stay here and get you somethin to eat. Enjoy the music. Laney Martin's back in town—I forgot to tell you. You and her can sit and visit. You can also meet Will's wife, Catherine. She's expecting a baby around the same time as my birthday."

Valentine didn't wait for her to say anything else. He smiled at her and Adam, then snapped the reins of the horse and clicked his teeth. "*Hyah.* Let's go, Penny."

Adam led Mary back into the warehouse, where she decided to set the serving table while he went back outside to see if Boaz needed any more help with the pig.

WITHIN THE NEXT HOUR THE warehouse had been creatively transformed by Mary into a much more inviting venue. She discovered several empty barrels in a corner of the warehouse, so she got Martin, who arrived shortly after Valentine left, to help her set them up as tables. They grabbed crates and whatever other things as they could find to use as chairs. It would be a welcome sight for partygoers, as no one would want to stand around outdoors very long on a day like this.

The enormous building was chilly, with its high ceiling, but it was not as cold as it was outside, and it would soon be more comfortable as it filled with warm bodies.

Had she not improvised those improvements for the guests, they would've likely been standing and eating at several long communal tables that would've been thrown together with long boards over crates.

Soon Emmanuel came downstairs so he could be ready to welcome folks as they arrived.

The gathering was far from pretentious, and yet nearly all of Beaufort's gentry came. The handful of men who had been at the meeting with Emmanuel were among the most influential, and deep pocketed, in the county. These were the men upon whose shoulders—and wealth—it would depend if the canal project would ever come to fruition. More realistically, the work would fall upon the shoulders of the slaves belonging to many of these men, but nevertheless, lending their laborers to such a task would mean those same laborers were unavailable to work at the jobs they were originally purchased to do.

The success of the project was entirely dependent on these civic-minded gentlemen.

When Laney Martin arrived with her brother and his wife,

Adam warmly remembered the party at Richard Rasquelle's estate where he had first met the girl. That was a very different affair—with a string trio and harpsichordist providing music to a formal garden party with a waitstaff, rather than a ragtag band of tavern musicians playing jigs in a dusty warehouse with barrels for tables and crates for chairs.

Regardless of where she was—warehouse or fine garden—to Adam she was the loveliest thing in all of Creation.

Naturally, Ellison Smythe, the Port Beaufort customs inspector, was an invited guest. When he showed up with his arrogant son, Francis, Adam was understandably annoyed. Francis was close to Adam's age but was spoiled rotten thanks to his frequently absent father's insistence on having servants meet his petulant son's every need. From what Adam had heard, though, the senior Smythe had tightened the reins a bit after his son's altercation with Adam the previous year.

As long as he stays the hell away from Laney, we'll be just fine, thought Adam. He knew Laney and Francis had been associates at least, if not friends, because of their families moving in the same circles. But Adam was thankful he didn't have to make a habit of fraternizing with the obnoxious brat.

After all the guests arrived, Emmanuel invited the Reverend Miller, who was also in attendance, to say the blessing. Then the party began.

EVERYONE LINED UP AT THE end of the long table with all of the food on it and made their way down either side. A large portion of the cooked pig had been brought in and placed on the table inside, and folks would "pick" out what they wanted, then move down the line to fill their plates with vegetables and cornbread.

Tall and lanky Ed Willis and straw-haired Fred Canady, who had served on board the *Carolina Gypsy* with Adam and Martin on their trip to Cuba, were put in charge of serving the drinks. Ricky Jones, whose dark features could easily let him pass as Adam's brother were it not for his English accent, was also there, but Emmanuel had given him fair warning about getting drunk, just as he had Martin, so the two of them split their time between visiting with guests and cleaning dishes.

The Martins and Adam's mother all sat together at one table. Adam would've liked to have joined them, but Emmanuel had him busy, along with the other employees of Rogers's Shipping Company, in making sure that all of the guests were having a good time and eating plenty.

Adam couldn't help but occasionally glance over to see how his mother was getting along with Laney and the Martins. He also couldn't help but keep an eye out to see if Francis Smythe was trying to drop in on their conversation. He was relieved that Francis seemed occupied talking with some of the other high-society young men who were there.

The musicians did help liven up the party. Adam couldn't imagine how dull the event would be if they weren't there, with everyone just standing around, an assortment of wooden and china plates in hand, eating and trying to mingle.

Finally, Adam was able to take a couple of moments to spend some time at the table with the Martins. His mother gave him her seat and said that Martin and Ricky could use some help with the dishes, as things were beginning to wind down. He was relieved to at least see a sincere smile on her face when she excused herself. It was the first time in recent memory that he could recall her genuinely appearing to have a good time. He was glad Valentine had made her stay behind. It was obviously just what she needed to rejoin the land of the living.

"You seem to be enjoying yourself, Miss Catherine," Adam commented.

Will chuckled. His wife blushed and held her hand over her mouth as she nodded while chewing a piece of cornbread.

"Don't forget," Will offered, "she's eating for two, you know. She certainly doesn't let me forget at any expense."

Catherine jokingly slapped her husband's shoulder. "This condition is full of surprises," she said. "Early on I had no appetite whatsoever. Now it seems I can't get enough to eat. Everything tastes so good!"

Laney playfully tipped her head to the side and said, "Except my cooking, right?"

Catherine's eyes grew big and she gasped, "Oh, Laney!"

Will lowered his head in mock shame, and Adam couldn't help but be amused at the situation.

"There's little doubt you make a genuine effort to feed us all well, sweet girl," said Will, "but there's a reason we've always needed Aunt Celie. Women in our family are hardly known for being good cooks."

"Will, Will, Will…" said Adam, shaking his head. "You ought to be ashamed of yourself. What a thing to say to your sister!" He was trying very hard not to smile.

Laney looked at Adam and gave a half grin as she reached over to lightly touch his hand, which was resting on top of the table.

"It's alright, Adam. I know I'm a terrible cook. And if I didn't know it a couple of days ago, I surely know it now."

Adam put his hand over the top of hers and patted it. He

then swallowed hard before responding, "You're... not a terrible cook. I wouldn't say that at all." He gave her hand a little squeeze. A jolt went through him. He wondered if she felt it as well.

At the very least she must've been flustered. Finally, she looked quickly at her brother and his wife for their reaction before slipping her hand away back into her lap. "It was really good of you to eat all of the breakfast I served you yesterday. I finally had some myself after you went outside to see Cyrus and, well, it was just awful."

"No, Laney," said Will, "it wasn't just *good* of him to eat all of what you served him yesterday morning, it was downright *heroic*. How he was able to muscle down those dry, overcooked grits *and* the burnt bacon I'll never know."

"Come on, Will. It wasn't that bad," said Adam. "It was actually fine. Just needed a little butter and salt."

"Pfft! You only say that because you fancy her," Will said.

Both Catherine and Laney were obviously shocked that he'd come right out and say that.

Adam inhaled sharply and felt a tiny bit embarrassed, but he knew it wasn't a secret to anyone that he had an eye for Laney. He was only surprised that Will seemed willing to publicly acknowledge it and not warn him to keep away from her.

"Well," said Adam, "perhaps the lovely company enhanced the flavor of the food." He winked at Laney playfully in an effort to lighten what otherwise might be an awkward moment.

Just then someone tapped on Adam's shoulder. He turned to see it was Ben, the guitarist from the tavern.

"I'm sorry to interrupt you, but do you think we can have a word?"

Adam raised his eyebrows and looked at the Martins in surprise before excusing himself to go talk to the man. He walked with Ben over to the staircase that led up to the living quarters and motioned for them to sit there to talk, out of the way of the guests.

"What can I do for you?" Adam asked.

"I hate to pull you away from your friends there, but I reckon we'll be leaving shortly, and I wanted to ask you something before we go."

"What's that?"

"I didn't realize you worked for a shipping company when we spoke the other night. I used to do this kind of work." He motioned around the warehouse.

"Oh really?"

Adam was wondering why this man pulled him away from a memorable moment with Laney Martin to talk about his work history. As he glanced across the room, he spotted Francis approaching Laney and her brother at their table. He wanted to jump up and fly across the warehouse to drive him away, but he fully realized that would make him look like a complete lunatic. He tried to turn his attention back to Ben but kept one eye on Francis.

"Yes, and I'm told you're close to the owner."

"Huh?" It took Adam a second to register what Ben had just said. Then he nodded, "Oh yeah, I reckon you could say that."

"See, like I mentioned before, I'm looking for a way down to South Carolina—Charleston. My sister lives down there, and so I thought I could work here for a stint and get together some money so I don't go down there empty-handed. I have all these little nieces and nephews that I want to take presents for, and to be honest, this music bit just ain't cuttin it."

Adam suspected he knew what Ben was getting at, but right now that was the last thing on his mind. He noticed Francis put his hand on Will's back, and they laughed as though they were lifelong friends. He wondered what in the world the two of them could be talking about. This was really very distracting.

Ben continued, and Adam made a halfhearted effort to listen. "Well, I was wondering if you might put in a word for me with your master. Tell him I'm looking for a temporary situation, and see if he'd be willing to help me out. I'm a hard worker. I'm happy to work twice as hard for half the pay, so long as it gets me to where I'm going."

Adam was moved by Ben's sincerity, but really, all he could think about was getting back over there to Laney's table.

"A temporary situation? What did you have in mind?"

"I was thinking maybe he can hire me as crew the next time he has a shipment going out, so long as it's going south."

"Hmm… It's not very likely he'd do that," said Adam. "He's real particular about who he lets work for him, but if he has any other odd jobs around here, I'll mention to him that you're looking for something."

He must have been very obvious in his desire to get back to his friends, because Ben looked over at the same table and said, "I'm keeping you from your lady friend. I apologize."

Adam was a little embarrassed that he had been so clearly uninterested and rude while this man was coming to him with a genuine need.

"It's alright. I do feel like I should get back over there soon, though. We can talk about this some other time if you like."

Ben nodded. "That's alright. Just tell him I'm happy with any job, long as there's money at the end of it." He grinned.

Adam nodded. He felt sorry for the man because he knew Emmanuel wouldn't hire him for shipping company work. Still, he didn't want to dash the man's hopes right away.

"Alright then. I'll have a word with him tonight, see what he says."

Ben reached out to shake hands with him. "Thank you. Bless you. I appreciate it, and I know my sister will, too. The sooner I can get to Charleston, the better."

Adam patted him on the shoulder and wished him well, then quickly went back over to where the Martins sat with Francis.

Anyone who could observe the two of them at that table would say there couldn't be a more stark contrast between Francis Smythe and Adam Fletcher. Smythe was tall, slender, and had light-blond hair—which he kept perfectly coiffed in the latest styles from England—fair skin, and pale-blue eyes. He wore fancy clothes imported from Europe that must have been tailored especially for him. His face was always, *always* clean shaven. In fact, so much so, one might wonder if he ever grew any facial hair at all.

Adam's wavy hair and dark features aside, he'd never had a tailored *anything* in his life, so his clothes nearly always fit him a little too long or a little too loose. Half the time he pulled his shoulder-length hair back into some kind of tie, but the other half of the time he left it loose, with a little bit tucked behind the ear. And it wouldn't matter if he had just shaved that morning; by afternoon the shadow of the dark beard lurking beneath the surface of his skin could almost always be detected.

While a woman's preferences might vary in terms of whether she likes fair-featured aristocratic types or tall, dark, and handsome rugged types, one clear advantage Adam had over Francis was his physique. Francis had never worked a day in his life and it showed, whereas Adam was muscular, especially across the upper body, from the manual labor he did working for Emmanuel.

"Who was that man?" Laney asked as soon as Adam returned to the table.

Adam looked back over his shoulder to see if Ben had already left. "Oh, his name is Ben. He's one of the musicians from the tavern."

"What did he want to talk to you about?" she asked.

"He's looking for some extra work."

"So are you going to help him?" asked Laney.

"I told him I'd mention it to Emmanuel, but I doubt he'll have anything for him."

He directed his attention across the table. "So, Francis, did you enjoy the dinner?"

Francis gave a reserved nod, then looked in Laney's direction as he answered, "Even those of us with more refined tastes can enjoy the rustic once in a while. Isn't that right, Rocksolanah?"

Adam rolled his eyes, but thankfully Francis didn't see him. *Nobody* called her by her full name except Emmanuel, and that was because he was more formal in his social graces with nearly everyone. What was Smythe trying to prove?

"It could be that some of us prefer the rustic to the refined sometimes," Laney countered with a sweet smile.

Francis gave a polite, deferential nod. "Perhaps," he said.

"It certainly allows us ladies, at the very least, to breathe a little easier," said Laney. "Isn't that right, Catherine?" She looked at her sister-in-law, who appeared to be increasingly uncomfortable after the large meal.

Catherine rested her hand on the top of her belly and nodded. "Indeed. Though I think I could breathe easiest if we returned to the estate so I can recline in the bed for a while."

"Understood," Will said. "I suppose we'll go then."

At that the Martins bade both Adam and Francis farewell, and they left the warehouse to return home.

Adam was always sad to part ways with Laney, but he was at

least relieved that the conversation with Francis ended without incident *or* serious insult.

Or so he thought.

Just as he was about to return to helping clean up the warehouse, Francis stopped him.

"Fletcher, a word?"

Adam turned towards him. "Hmm?"

"I hope we can put the foolishness of our youth behind us. I think we both behaved poorly when we were younger and, shall we say, a bit wilder?"

Adam wasn't sure what to say at first. He raised his eyebrows and responded, "I already have put it behind me. And I'm paying my debt now for what I did to you."

"I know," said Francis. "You appear to be doing fine for yourself. That's a pleasure to see. I suppose in some ways our little *disagreement* has led you to bigger and better things, wouldn't you say?"

Adam took a deep breath, then sighed. "I suppose you're right. Emmanuel always says Providence can be a funny thing."

Oh, there were so many things he could say to Francis—so many things he *wanted* to say—and yet Francis's observation was true. Had they not gotten into that fight outside the Topsail a year and a half ago, he'd still be at the tavern, he wouldn't have met many of those he considered his closest friends now, and most importantly, he wouldn't know his father *or* his grandfather.

In an effort to lighten a very awkward moment, Adam said, "So what? I suppose I should thank you for dishonoring my mother so I had an excuse to break your nose, huh?"

Francis didn't answer that question. He raised his eyebrows as if to say, *Who knows?* and gave a little shrug.

"I am happy in my position," said Adam. "I reckon I feel a little bit like Joseph."

Francis looked at him, confused.

"You know, Joseph? His brothers sold him into slavery because they hated him, but in the end it was because of that he was able to rise to great power and save his family from famine. How was it he put it? 'But as for you, you meant evil against me; but God meant it as good.'"

"Yes, well, I'm delighted our childish fisticuffs helped to usher you into your destiny."

Adam chuckled.

"But one thing, though," said Francis. "About Rocksolanah… I hope you wouldn't be so selfish and shortsighted as to try and win her affections."

Adam wrinkled his brow. He couldn't believe Francis had the nerve to try and comment on his relationship with Laney Martin.

"Listen, I'm not saying this to you as your adversary but rather as one of Rocksolanah's peers. I have little doubt that she fancies you a bit. It's been known to happen—the well-bred young lady being tempted by the fruit of a baseborn suitor. Maybe it's a little bit of the *rustic* charm that does it."

"Baseborn suitor?" Adam felt his blood beginning to boil. "Are you completely out of your mind? You realize where we are—this is my home, my place of employment, and I have no intention of standing here letting you insult me *and* try to dispense advice to me about my personal life."

Francis stood there rigidly and unaffected.

"You're right. I'm not the hothead I used to be. I've grown, I've seen more than you can imagine, and I'm not stupid. I won't get baited into another fight with you. You can keep calling me a bastard, but no matter how many times you say it, it doesn't make it true. Furthermore—"

"Fletcher," Francis calmly interrupted him, "it isn't my desire to fight with you. And I can assure you I am not trying to provoke you. I am only trying to encourage you to give serious consideration to the fact that you ought not toy with a young lady's emotions. If Rocksolanah fancies you, and yet you know you're not the best possible man for her, do the gentlemanly thing. Lead her not into temptation. Help her to preserve herself for someone who can give her everything she deserves—and she, no doubt, deserves the best of everything."

At that, Francis excused himself and left the warehouse.

Chapter Fourteen

THE PIG PICKIN HAD WRAPPED up about an hour before sundown. Once nightfall came the temperature would drop outside, and it would be less convenient for folks who had a good distance to travel home.

After everyone left the party, Emmanuel had his employees gather around, and he told them he'd volunteered them to do an informal survey of the area where the canal would begin a few miles northwest of Beaufort. The team would include Adam, Martin, Jones, and Ed Willis. Cousins Elliot and Joe Salter would stay behind with Boaz to work in the warehouse, since Boaz had promised the Martins he'd make some new barrels for them for salting pork. They would be needed when Cyrus and a couple of other hired hands did their annual hog killing in the coming week.

"All of you come gather 'round here, and let's look at the map." Emmanuel spread out a large piece of parchment on top of a crate.

"You'll enter the mouth of Harlowe Creek here." He pointed

to a place on the map. "Then you'll go north about a mile or so. You won't be able to travel any further, because see this here?" He pointed to a small line that tapered off. "It will get too shallow. Then it'll turn into pocosin. That's where the canal will begin."

"How long will it be?" asked Martin.

"That's precisely why I'm sending you out there," said Emmanuel. "Judging by the map, we're thinking it should require between two and three miles of dredging and tree clearing to allow clear passage from the Neuse to Topsail Inlet, but it may turn out to be more."

"But we're not to be doin any o' that, right, sir?" asked Ricky Jones. "'Cause it's filthy work, that."

Adam could see that his grandfather's patience with Jones was growing thin. As if it wasn't enough for Emmanuel having to deal with Martin's increasingly reckless behavior, he was now having to hear Jones's frequent complaining about whatever tasks the crew was assigned.

"Not this time, Jones," said Emmanuel. He smiled mischievously. "Not now, anyway. Though I reserve the right to keep you here next time the *Gypsy* makes a trip so you can be of assistance in the dredging efforts."

Jones raised his eyebrows in dismay and looked at Emmanuel in shock. Adam and Martin knew Emmanuel was just joking, so they laughed.

"Why aren't any of the other men from the meeting sending anyone out to help us do this?" said Martin. "I mean, we can do it ourselves of course, but I just don't see why it's all fallin on you, Emmanuel."

"I'm sure some of the others might be willing to send men out, but I'm trying to demonstrate good faith here in the project. I'm the only full-time shipping merchant in town now, and so obviously we stand to benefit from this canal as much as anyone might. Before I ask others to help out, I think it fair that I do my part. Don't you?"

Martin and the others nodded in agreement. Emmanuel was exceedingly fair. Some said he sacrificed too much in the name of good business. He'd say doing the right thing always pays off.

"Why are we going up there now rather than waitin till the weather turns a little warmer?" said Martin.

Emmanuel shrugged his shoulders and shook his head. "It's up to you, Mr. Smith. You're welcome to wait until the weather turns, so long as you don't mind contending with the water moccasins and other creatures waking up from their winter slumber."

"Right, mate," said Jones. "We'll go straight away then, won't we?"

The others all agreed and they decided they would meet back at the warehouse shortly after sunup on Monday morning. Depending on the direction of the wind, it might take anywhere from an hour and a half to several hours to get from the dock at Rogers's Shipping Company to the mouth of Harlowe Creek. They would take gear to make camp for the night and a Gunter's chain to measure the expected length of the canal.

In the meantime Emmanuel gave everyone Saturday off to get ready for Monday, since he didn't let his men work on Sundays.

LATER THAT EVENING ADAM RODE Emmanuel's horse down to the tavern. Ordinarily he'd walk, but it was horribly cold outside, so the sooner he could get there, the better. He was sleepy because of getting up so early that morning to help Boaz cook the pig.

He didn't stay at the tavern very long. He had a pint with

Valentine and talked to him about the day, then went upstairs to visit with his mother for a bit before returning to the warehouse. He told her how happy he was to see her enjoying herself at the party and that he hoped she would continue to be social whenever she had the opportunity.

When he finally returned to the warehouse, he made a beeline for his bedroom. Though he felt physically exhausted, he couldn't help but lay awake thinking about his conversation with Francis Smythe. He'd tried not to give it much thought after it happened, but now, in the solitude of his bed, he couldn't get away from what had been said. The part about Smythe calling him "baseborn," insinuating his illegitimacy, didn't even bother him anymore. He knew without a doubt that was a lie. What bothered him was Smythe's suggestion that he not pursue a relationship with Laney because he wasn't good enough for her.

There were so many things about what he said that unsettled him. First of all, even if Adam did pursue a relationship with Laney, he knew it would be a little more than two years before he would be free to fully commit to her. Legally, as an apprentice he was bound to his master until he was twenty-one years of age. And even though his master just *happened* to be his grandfather, he knew Emmanuel would insist he finish out his apprenticeship for the sake of completing all of his training. Not to mention Adam knew there would be little appeal for Laney to marry a man with no real property to call his own.

Yet Adam also knew that Laney cared for him. She seemed to keep him at arm's length, though—at enough of a distance to maintain propriety, but close enough that he could tell she wanted him in her life. And that's where things got complicated. Adam loved everything about Laney Martin. He'd be the first to admit he'd initially been drawn in by her beauty, but as he got to know her, he had become captivated by her sweet disposition, her sharp mind, and her independent spirit. But part of him did wonder if he was the best she could do. That's not to say he thought Francis Smythe would be a better choice, but maybe there was another young man out there who could offer her a brighter future.

Adam thought about his own family history compared to hers. His mother was born into a family of humble means, then orphaned as a young girl and raised by Valentine Hodges and his wife, Margaret, at the Topsail Tavern. She'd married his father in secret when she was only seventeen years old, and they were soon driven apart because of the dangers posed by his father's crazy, jealous uncle in Cuba.

And speaking of his family in Cuba, Adam might've been wealthier than the Martins could ever imagine if things had been different with his Spanish relatives, but then if things had been different, Adam's mother and father would have never needed to part ways, leaving Adam to be raised alone by his mother at the Topsail Tavern.

It was all so frustrating. When it came right down to it, Adam knew the only thing he could do was to just plow ahead at being the most successful he could possibly be. He knew he had a secure position in the shipping company, and especially with the new canal being built, that could greatly increase the amount of shipping business coming into Beaufort. Whether or not things were meant to be with him and Laney only time would tell, but for his part he was going to do his best to become the best man he could be.

And right now the best thing he could do was get some rest. The days ahead would be long and arduous.

Chapter Fifteen

SATURDAY WAS SPENT WITH ADAM and the others getting all of their things ready to spend a couple of days in the marsh up on Harlowe Creek. Sunday, as Emmanuel always insisted, the whole company was in church for services. Afterwards, they all went their separate ways until Monday morning. Adam decided to go spend some time at the tavern.

Martin, Jones, and Ed Willis said they were going to spend the afternoon playing cards—something Emmanuel didn't approve of on Sundays but didn't forbid—but Adam knew they were probably planning a wilder night than that.

It was a little unusual, only because Ed generally didn't partake in the same kinds of entertainment that Martin and Jones did, but Adam figured it must've been a spur-of-the-moment decision that came from the kind of boredom that plagued all young men in Beaufort when it was too cold to swim or fish or do the other things they usually enjoyed on a full day off from work.

Adam turned in early Sunday night so he'd not be too tired the next day. He'd learned from experience that traveling on little sleep was not pleasant, and traveling in the cold across a potentially choppy Newport River would be even worse.

When time came Monday morning for everyone to meet at the warehouse, Martin and Jones were the first to show up. Of course Adam was already there, since he only had to go as far as down a flight of stairs.

"Where the hell is Willis?" Boaz said to Martin and Jones. "Y'all need to get goin, 'cause winds are coming out of the northwest, so it's gonna be a long, rough trip."

"How are we supposed to know?" asked Martin.

"I'd wager he's passed out," said Jones. "I reckon he'll be needin the ol' hair o' the dog."

"Damnit!" said Boaz. "Leave him home then. He'll drag in eventually and Emmanuel can deal with 'em. He's near 'bout had it with y'all's constant drinkin. You're turnin into a bunch of damned good-for-nothin sots."

"Are you saying you just want the three of us to go, then?" said Adam, a little concerned not only about leaving one of their crew behind but also because cutting their team by a quarter would mean they all had more work.

"Yep. The three of you will just have to go on your own. I'm not losing help in the warehouse these next couple of days just because y'all are too irresponsible to make sure you all show up."

"You must be joking!" Adam challenged Boaz. They had a long history of butting heads, so this wasn't new, but it didn't usually end well. "Ed's a grown man. Why should we be expected to be responsible for him to show up for work?"

"Because you all are a team on this survey. If you can't even keep your team together now, then I worry about y'all out there in the marsh."

Adam was annoyed by Boaz's answer, but he tried to act as if he didn't even care.

"Fine," he said.

He grabbed up his satchel and his bedroll and then offered to help Jones carry the small trunk with the tools and camp implements on board.

Once they were all loaded up into the periauger, they readied the sails and were underway, headed west on Taylor Creek towards Gallant's Point and into the Newport River.

Before they made it past the town, Adam had an idea.

"Let's dock over there by the boatbuilders. I think I know where we can get us another hand—at least if you fellas don't mind splitting some of your pay with him. That way Emmanuel won't even have to know. We can drop him back off here before we get back to the warehouse tomorrow or the next day."

Martin and Jones liked the sound of that, and they were willing to give up a little bit of their pay to get another man to come along. The fact was it was dangerous to go into the marsh like that with a team of just three men. If one got hurt, they'd struggle to get the third man back and safely sail to town if weather conditions were less than ideal.

They all reckoned Emmanuel would've insisted they take another man had he been there, but he had gotten to where his arthritic condition was giving him a terrible time early in the morning, so it took him longer to warm up and come down to the warehouse than it did when he was a younger man. At the same time they also knew he would've never approved of them challenging Boaz's authority, since he essentially ran the warehouse these days.

"Who you goin ta get, mate?" asked Jones.

"That fella Ben—the guitarist at the tavern. He asked me to let him know if I heard about any odd jobs he could do. He's trying to save up money to get down to Charleston to see his sister, but Valentine is cheap, and so it's taking him a long time to make what he needs."

"Haha! Perfect," said Martin. "Good thinkin, Fletcher."

They tied up to the public dock near the boatbuilder's shop, and Adam quickly ran over to the tavern to find Ben. Within about ten minutes he was running back to the boat, Ben following close behind, still trying to stuff his own clothes into a bag on such short notice.

As they got underway, Ben thanked them all for giving him a chance and said he'd be happy to keep the whole thing quiet as long as they slipped a little bit of money his way once they got paid. The timing worked out nicely, since his trio didn't play on Monday nights anyway, and if they weren't back in time on Tuesday, Toby and James could get along without him.

Chapter Sixteen

THE TRIP TO HARLOWE CREEK was brutal. Sailing into the wind as they crossed the Newport River meant dealing with freezing temperatures beating against their faces and piercing through their clothing. It took them hours to travel just the ten-mile distance it was from the public dock at Beaufort to their destination.

They came with plenty of provisions. They would be making camp for at least one night, possibly two, as they worked their way into the interior of the pocosin, trying to ascertain the obstacles that would be in the way when the canal project did get underway. There were some landowners in the region, but their properties were few and far between and nowhere near where they would be working.

The only advantage to the bitter cold was that the creeping, crawling, and winged beasts that normally made the marshland and pocosins so dangerous were in hibernation or otherwise dormant. Adam was especially glad they wouldn't have to worry much about water moccasins as they stepped through the high grasses. His friends might have feared alligators more, but Adam always felt like they were easy enough to see to avoid, whereas snakes could slither up from out of anywhere.

After pulling the periauger up onto the eastern bank of Harlowe Creek and tying it to a tree, the men decided to work their way as far north as they could until they needed to turn back for nightfall. No official surveyors were with them, since precise measurements weren't necessary.

Martin and Jones already had some experience using a Gunter's chain. They explained how one length of chain—which consisted of a hundred long, straight links—equaled sixty-six feet, which meant eighty lengths of chain equaled one mile. Martin and Jones decided they would carry the chain forward while Adam and Ben held their position. Once they'd marked off that distance, Adam and Ben would cross the terrain, chain in hand, to meet Martin and Jones, and then they would be the ones to carry the chain forward. They would keep taking turns like this, and Ben would make notes in a little journal along the way.

The shoreline of Harlowe Creek was typical of every estuary in the region. The ground went from being a murky, muddy muck with sparse marsh grasses poking through and the occasional fiddler crabs scurrying past, to increasingly thicker patches of rushes and reeds that made it nearly impossible to see the ground. That, of course, presented a challenge to them as they tried to walk across it, since the marshland was pocked with serpentine channels of water. One never knew whether or not a step on what looked like solid ground might turn out to be wet, sticky mud.

There didn't appear anything too remarkable at first, though they did continually see vultures plunging down into the marsh off in the distance to the north of them.

"Lucky bastards," said Martin. "Must've gotten themselves some fairly fresh kill. It don't even smell like there's nothin dead out here."

Adam sniffed the air. Martin was right.

"It's probably 'cause of the cold, don't you reckon? Or maybe we're just not close enough to it yet."

"That's true," Martin agreed.

Knowing they'd make it over that way within the next few minutes, the four of them took bets about what unfortunate creature was being gobbled up by the winged scavengers. Adam said he figured it was some kind of large marsh bird, like a heron or a pelican. Martin guessed it had to be something more substantial, like an otter or a raccoon, since it was attracting so many vultures. Ben reckoned it was an ugly old possum, and Jones went so far as to say he thought it might even be a coyote or a red wolf.

As they got nearer, though, there was definitely a rotting smell, and it seemed to completely permeate the damp swamp air.

They had their answer of what it was soon enough. Martin was the first one to it.

"Good Lord," he said.

"What is it?" Adam called out.

Martin stood there dumbfounded.

Adam and the others did their best to traipse through the grasses and over narrow channels of marsh to get to where Martin was standing on the edge of a reedy bank. The vultures in the grasses nearby seemed unfazed by their approach, but as they got nearer, Jones made some noise, and they all left in a wild commotion.

It took Adam a moment to assess the situation. Martin still wouldn't say a word. Jones and Ben looked at each other in shock—they apparently understood what it was right away. Adam, on the other hand, was behind them and couldn't see yet what they were seeing. Then he noticed something in the grass. It was an old canteen with smeared blood dried on the top and across the front.

It must be a man, he thought. He caught up with the others as quickly as he could, and as soon as he saw what they were looking at, almost instinctively he backed up and looked down at his feet, lest he be stepping in some kind of filth.

There lay the corpse of a man that had been chewed up by scavengers. His death must have happened days or even weeks earlier, but Adam still couldn't help but feel like the very ground they were standing on was contaminated. He wondered what kind of diseases might ooze out of the decaying body and into the water that licked at the bank nearby with every high tide.

After a few seconds of silence, finally Jones spoke up. "What in the hell happened to 'em?"

"I'm not touchin him," said Martin.

As they all exchanged glances with each other, Adam said, "Don't look at me!"

Ben stroked at his chin but appeared determined to show his maturity around these young men. He tentatively stepped over to the body and examined it as best as possible without actually kneeling down or touching it in any way—which didn't amount to much of an examination. He looked around and said, "Anybody see a stick or a branch anywhere? I ain't touchin no corpse with my bare hands."

The three others looked around the immediate area but didn't find much. Then Adam's foot stumbled on something. When he looked down, he saw it was a walking stick. It must've belonged to the poor fellow rotting nearby. He reached down and picked it up and brought it over to Ben.

Ben examined the stick for a moment before using it to poke gently at the corpse's torso. The body was facedown in the wet marsh grass. Adam was sure all four of them were thinking the same thing: the corpse ought to be turned over so that they might be able to figure out what happened to the man, but they all dreaded to see the condition of his face and gut. It was bad enough to see that his ears and fingers were being picked apart by crabs, in addition to the work the vultures had done to get past the obstacle of the man's clothing.

"Just do it quick," said Martin. "Get it over with."

"Put that stick under there," said Jones, pointing to the corpse's arm, which was tucked under his side, "and wedge it under 'em a bit so you can turn 'em right over."

Ben looked at Jones with a little wince. Adam understood his sentiment exactly. None of them wanted to see that body turned over, but they knew it had to be done. They at least wanted to see if he had any kinds of obvious injuries, or if it was more likely that he died of natural causes or exposure.

It so happens that turning over a corpse with a stick isn't as easy as it might sound. It ultimately took not only Ben using the walking stick to apply leverage under the body, but also the other three using their boots to turn the whole corpse onto its back all at once.

The most ungodly smell was released into the air as they flipped him over. Once he was on his back, they were at least slightly relieved that the front side of his body actually wasn't as bad off as his back side. There was no question as to what killed the poor man. It was a stab wound in the center of his chest, just below the sternum. None of them had seen blood when the corpse was facedown, because it had obviously poured out of the wound and was absorbed quickly by the front of his clothing and the ground.

Speaking of clothing, he wasn't dressed in any finery. His clothes were quite common, in fact.

They wondered if this was possibly the result of some family feud on a nearby farm, but Martin pointed out that there were no families that he knew of within at least a mile or two from where they were standing, and that it was unlikely that a family feud would've ended way out there in the marsh.

After a largely fruitless debate about what it could have been and what it was unlikely to have been, Adam suddenly had a different thought.

"What about that couple that was attacked on the road to New Bern? Maybe everybody's been thinking those killers were headed north, but what if they were really headed south?"

Martin and Ben both nodded as they appeared to consider the possibility.

"Wait. What couple?" said Jones.

"You mean you haven't heard about it?" said Martin, incredulous.

Ben shook his head in lament as he began to explain. "It was in the paper. A husband and wife were traveling about ten miles south of New Bern—on the south side of the Trent—and a couple of bandits attacked them. The husband tried to fight them off before they attacked his wife, but one of the men knocked him in the head and killed him."

"What happened to the woman?" asked Jones. "Did they abuse her in any way?"

Adam shook his head. "No, I don't think so. Apparently the

men argued after the husband fell dead and then decided to just take off before anyone came along and discovered them."

"Yes," said Ben. "They just left that poor woman in the woods, bless her. They say she walked near 'bout two miles before she was rescued."

Jones was speechless.

The four of them stood there by the body for a moment before Martin said, "That was a terrible crime, but like Ben said, that happened almost ten miles south of New Bern. And that means it was about twenty miles northwest of here. It ain't like that's right down the road."

Adam nodded. "That's true. I was just thinking—what are the chances of there being a murdered man here and then there being a couple of people attacked not twenty miles up this same route? I don't know that that girl in New Bern has anything to do with this."

"What girl in New Bern?" Ben asked.

"Just last Monday there was a girl attacked right in town and left on the road that leads to the estate where she's bound as a servant," said Adam. "It wouldn't have made it in the paper yet, though."

"That's terrible," said Ben. "But why do you say it wouldn't have anything to do with this?"

"Just think about it," said Adam. "She was attacked and dumped off. I don't remember hearing that she was robbed. Anyway, she was just a servant girl—about my age, I think."

They all stood there contemplating the crime spree that was apparently taking place across the region.

Finally, Ben said, "But think about it—maybe this is what happened: What if this here fella was the first victim? And those bandits had come from that way?" He swung his arms back in the direction of Beaufort, then back around to where they were standing. "They'd have got to him first. Then a couple days later they'd have made it up to where that husband and wife were attacked. And since they didn't satisfy their lusts on that first woman, maybe they made it to New Bern and took that girl and attacked her. Who knows how far north they could be now?"

"That makes right much sense," said Martin.

"I agree, mate," said Jones. "But I just can't believe this fella's been out here in the marsh for more than two weeks already. There'd be nothing left!"

"Wait a minute," said Adam, "but who is this man? And if he was their first victim, why was he stabbed when the other fella just got knocked in the head? And on top of that, he doesn't even look like he's got anything to steal."

"Think, boy!" said Ben. "He don't look like it now, but if he had anything to steal, don't you reckon those bandits would've already taken it from him? How do you know they didn't rob him, then kill him? Look at him. He ain't even got a warm coat on. It's near 'bout winter. Don't you reckon he'd have been wearing more than this?"

"That's a good point," said Martin. "And I reckon those bastards didn't set out to kill the husband of that woman. Sounds like it just happened because he tried to protect his wife. Not to mention the whole reason they went after that pair in the first place was to rob them."

"Right, mate," said Jones. "And don't forget a couple of weeks ago the weather was a fair bit warmer. That's when the two o' you went to New Bern."

"Fine," Adam said. "But we're in the middle of nowhere. There's no town nearby, no farms real close. Why would he have been out here in the first place?"

"Hmm… Good point," said Ben. He twisted up his face in contemplation and scratched at the stubble on his chin, then suddenly looked like he had an idea. "It could also be that this man was their partner."

The others wrinkled their brows and looked at him, waiting to hear what he'd say.

Ben continued: "What if there were three of them to start off with, and then for some reason they got into a fight, and this one ended up with a knife in his chest?"

The others looked skeptical. That seemed like quite a leap but still plausible.

"These men are obviously criminals, right? They don't follow the same rule book you or I would follow," Ben said. "I think regardless of whether he was a victim of a robbery or their partner, all the pieces fit for this to have been the bandits' first victim. I think we need to hurry up and get on back to town and let the constable know about this—get him to come out to investigate it."

"You're right," said Adam. "Truth is we have no idea who this man is or who did this—and it could have something to do with those highwaymen. I reckon the more pressing question right now is, what do we do with him now that we found him?"

The four men all thought for a few seconds before Ben said, "We can't really put him back in the boat and carry him to town in the condition he's in. I think we ought to just give him a Christian burial right here as best we can."

"A Christian burial?" Martin chuckled. "Reverend Miller ain't here. Who's gonna give the sermon and all?"

"Don't be an idiot," said Adam. "He just means we ought to bury the man and say a prayer for him."

"Bury him with what?" said Jones.

"Yeah, we don't even have a shovel," Martin echoed Jones's concern.

"We need to figure somethin out, boys," said Ben. "It'd be indecent to just leave the poor man out here to rot in the elements."

They all thought for a few seconds.

Jones spoke up, "If we were at sea, we'd weigh his body down and sew him up, then gently drop him overboard."

"Of course you would," said Ben, "but we ain't got no weights, no shroud, no nothin to sink him down. Furthermore, you want to bundle this corpse up and put it on Mr. Rogers's boat to carry it out to sea? 'Cause we sure can't dump it here in Harlowe Creek."

"Fact of the matter is," said Martin, "he's already dumped out here in Harlowe Creek."

"That's true," said Adam. After a moment he said, "I think, given the circumstances, maybe we ought to just go on back to town and let the constable know what's happened, and he can decide what to do with the body. He might want to inspect it or something."

"Fletcher's right," said Martin. "And anyway, I sure as hell don't wanna anger his ghost by not doing the right thing in burying him, and I sure don't wanna be campin out here with a bunch of spirits."

"Ahhh!" Ben waved dismissively at Martin. "Spirits? You outta your mind, boy! You don't really believe that foolishness, do you?"

"Damn right I do," said Martin, standing his ground.

Ben looked at Jones, who was nodding in agreement with Martin, at which point Ben shook his head in disbelief.

"Don't tell me you too?" said Ben, looking at Adam.

Adam shrugged and smiled sheepishly. "I don't know about ghosts or spirits, but I do know I don't wanna stay out here tonight. Regardless of whether or not there are any spirits running around, there's obviously a killer on the loose."

THE FOUR OF THEM ENDED up using their pocketknives to check the man's pockets for personal items. Very curiously, the only thing they found was a silver pocket mirror. Ben picked it up and made a note of where they had found it in the journal they had brought, and he sketched a picture of it as well.

Before they left to pack up their camp and go back to the boat, Ben suggested they leave everything else as it was so the constable could see the way they'd found the corpse.

"We're not turning him over again, though," said Jones.

"No, I don't mean we need to turn him over," said Ben. "I just think we ought to leave everything right now just like we found it, and then hurry on back. I reckon we can make it to Beaufort before dark if we don't waste time."

The others agreed, and they all started walking back in the direction of the boat.

Adam suddenly felt the need to go back and get the canteen, but he also thought it would be best not to say anything about it. He quickly came up with an idea of how to do it.

When they all returned to the boat, Adam faked some stomach cramps.

"You don't look so good," said Martin.

Adam rubbed his hand over his belly and extended his back to show his "discomfort."

"You alright, mate?" said Jones.

At first Adam nodded. He then quickly grabbed his satchel and jumped out of the boat and started running into the marsh.

"Where you goin, Fletcher?" said Martin.

"Where do you think?" Adam yelled in response.

He kept running until he was out of sight, then crossed over to where the corpse lay. He quickly grabbed the canteen and stuffed it into his satchel. It made it way too bulky. He had too much in there, so he took the canteen out and rearranged things.

He decided to leave behind his cup and plate, as well as most of the newspaper he had carried along in case nature really did call, and he folded the remaining bit of newspaper over the canteen and stuffed it into the satchel.

When he returned to the boat, he feigned great relief over having *relieved* himself, and the other three were none the wiser to what he had done.

Chapter Seventeen

THANKFULLY, THE SAME WINDS THAT had brutally beaten against their faces on the way to Harlowe Creek were at their backs on the return trip. It took them under two hours to bring the periauger back to the public dock to let Ben out before the other three returned to the warehouse.

"I don't reckon Emmanuel will pay us everything yet for the survey, since we didn't get to finish," said Adam, "but as soon as we have the money, we'll get you your part."

Ben looked a little frustrated, but he nodded. "I understand. Things sure turned out strange today, didn't they?"

Martin inhaled sharply and sighed. "Yes, they surely did." He thought for a second, then said, "You know what? I'll just go ahead and pay you your part for this. I'll worry about getting paid from Emmanuel later. I feel like this is sort of my fault anyway that you had to come with us instead of Ed Willis. He ain't really used to knockin as many back as me and Jones."

Ben shook his head. "Naw, that's not necessary. You can just square up with me later."

Martin held out a few coins. "No, you go on and take these. A worker's worth his wages."

Ben smiled humbly and nodded his head in gratitude. "I do appreciate it."

He shook Martin's hand, then Adam's and Jones's, then climbed out of the boat and scurried back over to the tavern.

Adam and the others were docking at the warehouse just moments later, but no one was working inside.

"Damn Boaz!" said Martin. "And all that fuss he made today about needin to work on those barrels!"

He and Adam and Jones didn't bother unloading the boat, but Adam did bring his satchel inside.

They all three went upstairs to the living quarters, where they found Emmanuel and Boaz sitting at the table in a somber mood.

"What's going on here?" asked Adam.

"You all are already back?" Emmanuel said softly. "Did they tell you?"

The three wore puzzled expressions and looked at each other.

"Tell us what?" Adam asked.

"You haven't heard?" said Boaz. "Then why are y'all back?"

Adam crossed the room and pulled up a chair at the table. Martin and Jones followed suit.

"Ed Willis is dead," said Emmanuel.

No one said a thing.

This can't be happening, thought Adam. *This really can't be happening.*

"Not long after y'all left this morning, I sent Elliot over to wake Ed up… get him over here … 'cause of not bein here when y'all left to go do that survey."

Boaz took a deep breath. He looked like he was struggling to string his thoughts together into complete sentences.

"There weren't no answer at Ed's house. Elliot figured he must be passed out real good, so he went around the back—you know, 'cause the room he sleeps in is on that side of the house— he looked in the window, and Elliot weren't in his room."

"Where was he?" asked Martin.

"He went back 'round to the front door," said Boaz. "He tried to open it and it was unlocked, so he went on inside. Elliot was laying right there on the floor near his table, dead."

"Oh God!" said Martin.

"What happened?" said Adam.

Boaz started to answer, but it was apparent he was getting choked up, because he swallowed hard.

In a quiet voice Emmanuel said, "He had been stabbed here." Emmanuel made a stabbing motion against the top left part of his chest. "Elliot found him in a pool of his own blood."

"No," said Jones. He drew his head back in suspicion, then gave a little laugh. "What are you two on about? This must be some kind of joke… Ain't it?"

Emmanuel shook his head slowly. "I wish it were, Jones. I truly wish it were."

"What the hell?" said Martin. "Who would kill Ed Willis? He don't even do nothin bad! He's always been such a nice fella. He don't even get into half the wild mess that Jones and I do."

Emmanuel folded one hand on top of the other on the table. "We do not know exactly what happened, but we do know there were some cards on his table, and some had been knocked on the floor. One might say it looks as if he was gambling and his opponent robbed him for his winnings."

"How much winnings could he have had?" said Martin. "Ed Willis ain't exactly rich!"

Through all of this Adam couldn't think of a single thing to say. He was too busy thinking about how it was Ed Willis in Havana who had, without hesitation, gone into Eduardo's fortress with him to try and rescue Martin, Santiago, and Drake. It was Ed Willis who had driven the horse cart that gave him and his father a getaway from that place. And it was Ed Willis who had told him what he'd need to do to stop his father's bleeding, and even gave him his own belt to fasten around Santiago's arm.

Ed Willis had only met him for the first time on that trip to Havana, and yet he never hesitated to try and help him—or anyone who needed help—however he could. Of all people, why did this happen to him?

While they all sat there in silence, Adam was sure that Martin and Jones were wondering the same thing he was: When do we tell them about what we found in the marsh?

He didn't have to wonder long. Boaz came back to his earlier question.

"If y'all hadn't already heard about Ed Willis, then why are you already back?"

Jones looked down at the table. Martin looked at Adam. Finally, Adam realized he would have to be the one to provide an answer.

"We found something out in the marsh. We thought we better let the constable know."

Emmanuel wrinkled his brow. "What was it?"

"A body. It was a man. He'd been stabbed, too," said Adam.

"In the chest, but down here." He tapped his chest just below his sternum.

"Did it look like it happened recently?" asked Emmanuel.

"We don't think so," said Adam.

"Maybe a week or so ago," said Martin. "Who knows?"

They spent the next twenty minutes telling Emmanuel and Boaz about everything that happened and what they saw.

Emmanuel let out a soul-weary sigh. "Yes, the constable should know, but I need to rest first. I don't think I'm quite up for seeing anybody else just now."

He got up from the table and slowly made his way over to his room and closed the door.

Adam felt so sorry for his grandfather. He knew not only was he grieving over this recent tragedy but also that he was physically suffering with the worsening pain from his arthritis. It occurred to him Emmanuel might be so upset that he wouldn't bother with the fire that heated his room, so Adam quietly got up and went over to the room to tend to that for him and left the others talking at the table in the sitting room.

Chapter Eighteen

O N TUESDAY MORNING NO ONE was quite sure what they should be doing. Adam, Martin, and Jones had thought they'd be out surveying, but those plans obviously changed. Boaz, Elliot, and Joe had thought they'd be working in the warehouse—with Ed Willis—on the barrels for the Martin estate, but that also wasn't happening, since Elliot and Joe had gone up to Portsmouth Island to inform his family of his death.

Adam was always the last one to wake up—and it was usually because of hearing Boaz and Emmanuel shuffling around. When he realized he'd slept in until eight o'clock, he was alarmed. It took a few seconds for the fog to clear out of his brain enough for him to remember the events of the previous day. Then he was even more worried. Emmanuel never did go see the constable the night before—in fact, he never came out of his room. And it wasn't like Boaz to let him sleep in.

He quickly threw off the covers and got up out of bed. He went out of his room, through Boaz's room and the kitchen, and then he saw Boaz at the table, writing something on a piece of paper.

"Where's Emmanuel?" Adam asked.

"Still in bed," said Boaz.

"Is he alright?"

Boaz shrugged but was still looking down at the paper in front of him. "Can't really say. Haven't been able to talk to him."

"But you've checked on him, right?"

Boaz looked up, annoyed. "Of course. He ain't dead or anything. He just don't feel like gettin up, I reckon."

Adam narrowed his eyes in frustration at Boaz and strode across the sitting area towards Emmanuel's room. He gave the heavy oak door a light knock, but there was no answer. He slowly pushed the door open and peered into the room.

"Emmanuel?"

His grandfather made no answer. He was lying on his side, wrapped up tightly in his covers. Adam quietly entered the room and approached his bed.

He lightly tapped Emmanuel on the shoulder. "Emmanuel."

Finally, the old man stirred a little bit. He opened his eyes and saw Adam standing in front of him.

"Are you alright?" asked Adam.

"Adam." Emmanuel reached his arm across his body and took hold of his grandson's hand. "Son, will you please prepare me a cup of willow bark tea?"

"Of course," said Adam. "Can I bring you anything else?"

"Is there anything to eat?"

Adam shrugged. "I don't even know. As soon as I woke up and saw you weren't up yet, I came right in here. I can fix you something, though."

Emmanuel gave him a weak smile. "Thank you, son. Any simple thing would be fine."

"Are you hurting really bad?"

Emmanuel gave a slight nod. Adam could see that it was difficult for him to move his head. "The pain in my back is nearly unbearable."

"I'll go fix you something to eat and some of that tea. I'll be back in just a little bit."

As Adam started to leave the room, Emmanuel called out to him.

"Oh, Adam, one more thing. Please tell Boaz he must go see his cousin. I was too poorly to get out last night, and I'm afraid my condition isn't much improved today."

When Adam returned to the sitting room, he told Boaz what Emmanuel had said. His grandfather had been referring to Constable Lawson Squires, who just happened to be Boaz's cousin.

"I was already figurin on doing that," said Boaz. "I need to finish this first," he added, pointing at the paper he had been scribbling on in front of him.

Adam wrinkled his brow in curiosity at Boaz as he crossed the room into the kitchen. "What is that?"

"I'm tryin to make a list of all the things y'all said yesterday. I don't want to forget anything."

Adam called back into the room, "Oh well, I guess I should have mentioned that I can get you some notes together about that. In fact I already have some, but I just need a few minutes before I can get them together. I'm making Emmanuel some food and willow bark tea right now."

He could hear Boaz groan from the next room.

"I wish you'd have told us you had notes before I started writing all this," Boaz complained.

Adam thought about the fact that he didn't have the notebook. It was with Ben down at the tavern. He'd have to quickly go down there and get it from him and bring it back so that Boaz could take it to Constable Squires.

He quickly disappeared into his room and got dressed before he whipped up Emmanuel's breakfast and took it in to him. No sooner had he done that, he left the warehouse and told Boaz he'd be back shortly with the notes.

Now he had to get to the tavern fast and just pray that Ben would be around.

Chapter Nineteen

ADAM TOOK EMMANUEL'S HORSE TO the tavern so he could get there and back quickly. He barely took time to tie the poor creature to the hitching post before he ran inside.

"Mama," he said. "Do you know if that fella Ben Hamilton is here?" He sounded out of breath and quite dramatic.

Mary was carrying a tray with plates of food to a table. She shrugged at her customers and rolled her eyes at Adam.

"Well, good morning to you too, son," she said to him as she placed the plates in front of the two men at the table.

Adam stood impatiently at the bar and waited for her to finish with them so she could come over and speak to him.

When she finally did, Adam said, "So is he here?"

Mary wrinkled her eyebrows at him and shook her head. "I heard about Ed Willis."

Adam nodded impatiently. "Yeah, I know. It's terrible, but have you seen Ben? I need to talk to him."

"How in the world am I supposed to know? You need to ask Valentine." Mary gave Adam a look that made it clear she was disappointed in his callous response to her mention of Ed Willis.

"I'm sorry," said Adam. "I just don't have time to talk about that right now. This may be related to that, though."

Mary tsked at him and shook her head. "Go on. Talk to Valentine, then."

"Fine, I will. Where is he?"

Just then Valentine came through the door from the kitchen.

"Speak of the devil," said Mary. "Adam needs to talk to you," she said to Valentine.

She gave a quick wave good-bye to her son before returning to take care of her tables.

"I heard about Ed Willis. You doin alright this morning?" said Valentine.

"Well, I'm alive anyway," said Adam. "I need to talk to Ben Hamilton. You seen him?"

"Sure did," said Valentine. "He left first thing this morning as a matter of fact."

Adam wrinkled up his brow. "What do you mean he left? Did he and the other men check out?"

"No, the other two are still here. It was just him who left."

"That makes no sense," said Adam. He wondered if Valentine had possibly confused Ben with either Toby or James, the other musicians.

"I don't know whether it makes sense or not. All I know is their room is paid for through Friday, so it makes no difference to me whether one is stayin in there or three."

Adam turned his head and looked behind him towards the

door. He needed to get back to the warehouse with that journal of notes and the pocket mirror. Hopefully Ben had remembered to leave them for him in his room.

"Well, do you know if he left anything for me here?" asked Adam.

Valentine looked at him in bewilderment.

"Why would he? Of course he didn't leave nothin for you here—least not with me. Mighta left something with those two fellas upstairs, though."

Adam wasted no time turning the corner and flying up the stairs to the hallway that housed the guest rooms. There were only three rooms up there, and one of them belonged to his mother, so there were only two for him to check.

He gave a sturdy knock on the first door and there was no answer, so he went to the last room on the hall. *I should've known they'd be in this one*, he thought. It would have been unlikely for Valentine to put them in the room right next to Mary.

The musician named James answered the door. Adam didn't know his last name. He'd never learned it when he first met Ben and Toby. He was a very slight man, small, with greasy black hair and eyes black as coal, and a shadow on his face from the whiskers that were poking through all over it.

"Good day, sir," said Adam. "I know you may not remember me, but I came here early yesterday morning and asked Ben to—"

"Nay, lad. I cannae say that I do," James interrupted, shaking his head. "Dead ta the world yesterdee marnin t'was I."

Adam chuckled and gave a nod. He'd never heard the man speak before, so he was a little surprised by his accent. He'd assumed he was from the same place as Toby or Ben, but he was obviously not, though Adam couldn't decide for sure the exact origin of his brogue.

"Yes, sir. I understand," he told him. "Listen, I'm trying to find Ben—or at least find out if he left anything here for me. He had a couple of things that he was holding for me."

James shook his head. "I know not where he is nor if he left nothin. Seen him last night, I did, an' we all played some fair tunes, but I dinnae remember anathin after that."

"Do you at least know where he went?"

"Nay, tho' I recall 'im sayin he come into a wee bit o' luck and was on 'is way ta Charleston."

Adam lowered his head and thought about what James had said. It took him a second to understand all of it, as his manner of speaking was so different, but finally he decided to ask just once more, "And you don't think he left anything for me here, then?"

James turned back and looked into the room. "I dinnae see a thin' for ye. Took all that was here, he did. Perchance me chum Toby knows more than I. Ya might ask him tanight."

Adam gave him a single nod and said, "I'll try to do that. Thank you, sir."

Tonight, thought Adam. *That's no good. I need to get that notebook and silver mirror to Boaz now!* He knew there was no use in discussing it further with James, though.

He went back downstairs and spoke to Valentine once more before he left.

"If you hear anything about Ben, or when Toby gets back, if he says anything, would you please, please let me know somehow? It's important."

Valentine nodded. "Will do."

ADAM KNEW HE BETTER NOT go back to the warehouse without those notes, and since he didn't have the original notebook he briefly considered going to Moore's Mercantile to buy a new one. That idea was quickly scuppered, however, when he realized he hadn't brought any money with him. He was thankful in a way that the decision was out of his hands.

What choice would he have now but to tell Boaz about Ben coming to help the day before? He hated to do it—and it was precisely what he had hoped to avoid—but this whole business had gone far enough. Things were even more serious now with Ed Willis's murder.

As he rode the horse back to the warehouse, he thought about how frustrating Ben's sudden departure was, although he could understand it, considering how anxious he was to get down to Charleston to see his sister.

When he got back, he explained to Boaz about Ben and how they had brought him along to Harlowe Creek. He explained how Ben was assigned the journal to take notes in, and he had been the one who brought the silver mirror back to Beaufort to show the sheriff or the constable.

Surprisingly, Boaz wasn't even mad. In fact, he apologized to Adam.

"I reckon I forced y'all into it, and I'm sorry about not lettin one of the other fellas go. But I declare, between Martin's and Jones's foolishness lately and Ed Willis not showin up, I'd about had it." He lowered his head and stared at the floor. "Of course we know now why Ed won't there."

"I understand," said Adam. "I should have said something about it yesterday, but I didn't know how y'all would take it—after everything that had happened and all."

"What do you remember about that silver mirror?" Boaz asked.

"Well, like I mentioned, it was small." He opened his right

hand and rubbed his palm with the fingers of his left hand. "It was no bigger than this—and it fit in his pocket."

"Do you think it was real silver?"

Adam thought for a moment before he answered. "I reckon it probably was. You could see where it was tarnishing down in the grooves of the engraving."

"What was engraved on it?" asked Boaz.

"Let me think…" Adam rested his elbow on the table and pressed his forehead against his fingers. "What are those flowers called? They're purple—they smell real good, and they're all in a little bunch…" He quickly tapped his fingers across the table, deep in thought. "Hyacinth! I was trying to think of it. It was an engraving of hyacinth blossom, like this." He took the pencil and paper that Boaz had been using to make notes, and he made a very rough sketch of the design.

Boaz looked it over and then folded up the paper and stuck it in his pocket.

"Fine. I reckon I'll go on and see my cousin now, tell him what we know."

All of a sudden Adam remembered something.

"Wait a minute!" he said. He got up and dashed into his bedroom, then returned with the satchel he had been carrying to Harlowe Creek.

"I forgot I had taken this." He pulled the bloodstained wooden canteen out of his bag. "We found this near that man's body. There are initials on it." He pointed to the letters that were painted on the side.

Boaz was slow to take the canteen from his hands, careful not to touch it where it was stained. Adam realized that he had grabbed it in such a hurry the day before that he hadn't thought much about the blood dried on the thing, but thinking back on it, that was only because it had been so much less repulsive than the rotting corpse they had found.

"And you just now remembered this?" Boaz asked. "This is fairly important, don't you reckon?"

"You're right," said Adam. "It is real important. I just didn't think about it before. Remember, I was surprised to sleep so late this morning, and with Emmanuel so bad off, this canteen just wasn't the first thing on my mind."

Boaz nodded. "I understand." He wrapped the leather strap that hung from the canteen around it, then grabbed a cloth sack and stuffed it inside. "If nothing else, maybe those initials will help."

"Lord willing," said Adam.

Chapter Twenty

WHEN BOAZ LEFT THE WAREHOUSE, Adam checked in on Emmanuel once more. The old man was wrapped up warmly in his bed and seemed to be resting peacefully, so Adam thought it would be a good time to go see Laney and her brother and Catherine. He wanted to tell them about everything that had happened in the last couple of days in case the word hadn't gotten out to them on Lennoxville Point.

As he exited the living quarters and was about to go downstairs to leave the warehouse, he paused, and for the first time he wished he could lock the door, but he couldn't, because he was certain Boaz didn't have a key with him. *Maybe I should just wait until he gets back*, Adam thought.

He got about halfway down the stairs before he turned to go

back up. In a stroke of divine timing, Martin came into the warehouse just as Adam was about to return to the living quarters.

"Where you headed, Fletcher?" Martin called up the stairs.

"Nowhere, actually," said Adam. He went back down to the bottom of the stairs to talk to him. "I had thought I'd go out to your cousin's place to make sure they know about what all has happened, but then it dawned on me that I'd better not leave Emmanuel here alone with the place unlocked, and I doubt Boaz has a key with him."

"Go on," said Martin. "I'll stay here. I ain't doin nothin else today, anyway. I was goin to see if y'all had heard anything."

"Boaz has gone to find the constable."

"I thought Emmanuel was gonna do that last night," said Martin.

"He's real bad off with that arthritis. He's in bed and has been since late yesterday."

Martin looked concerned. "Really? I've never known him to be bad off like that."

Adam nodded. "I know. Me neither, but he's hurting real bad, and I guess this cold weather isn't really helping."

"Were you able to see Ben this morning?" Martin asked.

Adam realized his brain must have been in a fog. It had not even occurred to him to tell Martin what he had learned.

"No," he said. "I found out from Valentine this morning— Ben is gone."

"What the hell?" said Martin. He was visibly shocked and angry.

"According to that other fella, James, just before Ben left this morning he said he'd come into some luck and was heading on down to Charleston."

"Luck my ass!" said Martin. "The only luck he came into

was me being such a damned fool that I paid him out of my own pocket yesterday. Why would he have any reason to stick around after that? We ain't even gotten paid for that job yet, and who knows when we will now with all these murders happenin everywhere?"

Adam's face fell. "I had forgotten about that—I mean that you went ahead and paid Ben."

"Well, I damn sure haven't forgotten about it," said Martin. He kicked the side of the staircase.

Adam didn't want to tell Martin that not finding Ben also meant he had not been able to get the notebook *or* the pocket mirror. At this point he just wanted to get over to see Laney and make sure they knew what was going on.

"Listen, just stay here with Emmanuel, alright? I'm going to your cousin's place now. Boaz should be back directly."

Martin nodded. "Fine. I'll see you later."

ADAM CLIMBED ON THE BACK of Emmanuel's horse again and left for Laney's place. He rode out to Lennoxville Point as fast as he could and didn't slow down until he got to the hitching post in front of Laney's house. No one was outdoors, which was unusual to see. Usually Cyrus or Violet, or even Aunt Celie, would be outside doing something.

Adam went right around to the riverfront side of the house and ran up on the porch and pulled the cord to ring the bell.

Will answered. "Adam, what a surprise. Come on in." He motioned for Adam to enter.

They went into the parlor, where Catherine sat near the window working on needlepoint, and Laney was sitting nearby on the settee, reading a book.

Adam removed his hat and greeted them all.

"Have a seat," said Will. "It looks like you've been in a race."

Adam sat in a large green velvet chair next to the settee. "I feel like I have," he said. "Did y'all hear about Ed Willis?"

Will crossed the room and sat in a chair near his wife. "What about him?"

They haven't heard. Adam did not like having to be the one to tell them about it, but he knew that he had to, especially considering how far they lived from town. Who else would've told them?

Adam took a deep breath, then quickly sighed. "He was murdered."

Will, Catherine, and Laney all reacted in total shock:

"What?"

"When did this happen?"

"Do they know who did it?"

Adam shook his head. "No. All we know is, night before last—Sunday night—he was apparently at home playing cards. He had been with Martin and Jones earlier that evening. At some point he went home and got into another game. Then somebody stabbed him."

"Oh Lord, not again," Catherine said under her breath.

She was clearly affected strongly by the news. She winced and looked at her husband, then excused herself. Will gave her an understanding nod and told her to go lie down for a while and rest. Laney was not going anywhere, though. She clearly wanted to hear all about what had happened.

"When did you find out?" said Laney.

"Well, we didn't find out until we got back from Harlowe Creek yesterday evening. We had gone up there to do an informal survey for Emmanuel but ended up having to come back because of something that happened up there."

Will gave Adam a puzzled look.

"That's another story," said Adam. "I'll get to that in a minute."

Will had no choice but to wait and listen as Adam continued.

"See, yesterday morning Ed Willis was supposed to have come with us to do the survey, but he didn't show up. Since he'd been out with your cousin and Ricky Jones the night before, everyone figured he must've just been sleeping off his drink, but then Boaz sent Elliot over there to wake him up, get him into work, but Elliot found him dead on the floor near his table, stabbed in the chest."

Laney closed her eyes and shook her head. "I declare! What is this world coming to?"

"I don't know about the world," said Adam, "but seems to me this territory's got some real problems."

"First, there was that poor woman who saw her husband killed by those bandits, then there was that girl in New Bern, and now Ed Willis!" Laney shook her head in dismay. "Seems like criminals are running wild all over the place."

"Well, you ain't heard all of it yet," said Adam. "Remember how I was saying that we came back early from Harlowe Creek?"

Will and Laney both nodded.

"The reason we came back was we found a corpse out there. A man. He'd been stabbed, too."

Laney wrinkled her brow in concern. Will sighed.

After a moment Will said, "I hate to ask, but did it look like he'd been there long?"

Adam gave him a look to indicate that it would be best not to elaborate, then said, "I think a few days at least."

"Hmph."

Will didn't ask for more information, although Adam knew he probably would have, had Laney not been present.

"The reason I came out here was just to let y'all know," said Adam. "Y'all need to keep an eye out. Keep your doors locked. And none of y'all should be traveling alone or on unknown roads."

"Tell me something," said Will. "Was there anything about the body y'all found yesterday that gave any indication of who he was?"

Adam nodded. "We think so, maybe. There was a wooden canteen near his body that had some initials on it, and on his person there was a silver pocket mirror."

"What were the initials?" Will asked.

"I think it said RJ, but we aren't even sure if the canteen belonged to the man, or if it belonged to the killer, or who."

"And you said there was a mirror," said Will.

"Yes, it was in his pocket. It was pretty, but I reckon it was awfully feminine for a man to be carrying it."

"True enough," said Will. "You wouldn't catch me carrying such a thing."

"Did it have any initials?" said Laney. "I know my pocket mirror is engraved with AM. It was my mother's. Her name was Alice."

Adam shook his head. "No, I don't remember seeing any initials on that. But it was engraved with a hyacinth blossom."

"A hyacinth?" Will asked. "Are you sure?"

Adam nodded.

"That's very interesting," said Will. He looked as if he was suddenly in deep thought about what Adam had just said.

"What is it?" Laney asked.

Adam was wondering the same thing.

"The woman who was robbed south of the Trent—didn't I tell you what her name is?"

Adam and Laney both shook their heads.

"I don't think you ever mentioned their names," said Adam.

"So then you don't know her first name?" said Will. "Oh, no I don't suppose you would know. Their names weren't in the papers at all. They have been keeping it secret as a safeguard for the poor woman."

"What was her name?" said Laney.

"Her name was Hyacinth—Hyacinth Dudley," said Will. He turned his attention towards Adam. "And I'd say that mirror you all found on that corpse might well have been hers."

Adam wrinkled his brow. "Her name really was Hyacinth? I never met anyone with that name before."

Will nodded. "I know. Neither had I, but that's her name."

"But hyacinth is such a pretty flower. It might just be a coincidence that one was on the mirror," said Laney. "I would think it'd be lovely to have a mirror engraved with hyacinth blossoms. They smell like perfume."

"They are lovely," Adam agreed, "but your brother is right. That's awfully curious how there'd be a dead man in the marsh along Harlowe Creek who'd been stabbed, and who had on his person a silver mirror with a hyacinth blossom engraved into it, and some miles to the north a woman and her husband were robbed and the husband was murdered, and the woman's name was Hyacinth. What if she uses the flower like you use your initial?"

"There's only one way to know for sure," said Will. "We need to talk to somebody up in Craven County who would know."

"Who would that be?" said Adam.

"I know her family's attorney," said Will. "I could find out from him, but it would take a few days to go there and get back, and I really don't want to leave these ladies alone with a killer on the loose."

"I understand," said Adam. "How about if I go? I can get your cousin to come with me."

Laney looked worried. "I don't know that I like the idea of you traveling that distance right now with a killer on the loose."

Adam tilted his head to the side and flashed his dark eyes as he smiled at her.

"That's awfully sweet that you're concerned, but I'm much more concerned about y'all being here without your brother—especially given your sister-in-law's condition."

Laney sighed, then gave him a weak smile and a nod. "I suppose you're right," she said.

Adam did have one question for Will. "Do you think that attorney friend of yours would be willing to talk to me? He doesn't know me."

"He will," said Will as he stood from where he was sitting and crossed the room to sit at the writing desk. He pulled a sheet of paper from the drawer, along with a quill pen and drying powder. The jar of ink was already on the desk. "I'll write a letter to send with you. I'll explain the situation and instruct him to provide any pertinent information in return correspondence, unless he prefers to send a messenger. The most important thing is that we make this information available to him *and* the sheriff in Craven County."

As Adam waited for Will to write the letter, he noticed that Laney seemed very concerned. He moved from his chair to sit next to her on the settee.

"Don't worry about me," he whispered to her. "I can take care of myself."

She nodded and gave a tense smile, but Adam could tell that it wasn't sincere, that she was just putting on a brave face, because she looked sad in spite of the turned-up corners of her mouth. Her eyes looked a little watery, almost like she was on the edge of tears.

Adam reached over and gave her hand a gentle squeeze, and after a second she squeezed his back. She appeared to be comforted and demurely lowered her eyes.

Adam smiled at her and then stood and crossed the room to stand near her brother at the desk.

No candle was lit in the room, so Will took the candlestick that was kept on the desk and he lit it over in the fireplace along the same wall. He brought it back over to the desk and then used it to heat his sealing wax to seal the letter.

"Take this," he said, handing the letter to Adam. "You'll find him at the address I've written here." He pointed to some writing on the outside of the folded letter. "It's only a few blocks from my own house, and you're welcome to stay at my house while you're in town. Just tell Charles Jr. what I've sent you for."

"And check on Aunt Celie for me," Laney said. "Tell her I miss her terribly. That we're about to starve on account of my sorry cooking."

Adam looked back at her and laughed. "I don't know if I ought to tell her all that."

"If she wants to come back," said Will, "and I doubt she will, but if she wants to, it's fine with me if you bring her back here. I know she worries about Laney, and when she hears about all that's happened here she might very well want to return."

Adam nodded. "Understood."

"How will y'all go there?" Laney asked.

Adam gave a little sigh. "I reckon we'll go in Emmanuel's

periauger again. Seems like the safest thing to do, especially now. If it came right down to it, I'd rather deal with half-drunk pirates than murderous highwaymen any day."

Laney looked concerned that Adam would make light of the situation by saying something like that, but Will just chuckled.

"I agree with Adam. At least we know a thing or two about pirates, don't we, Fletcher?"

Adam crossed the room back over to where Laney had stood near the settee.

"Don't worry about us. Just pray that we'll have safe travels," Adam told her. "And we'll be back before you know it."

At that he gave her a wink and a smile. He then took the letter that Will had given him and returned to the warehouse.

Chapter Twenty-One

"I RECKON YOU NEED TO go on home and pack your things," Adam said to Martin as he strode back into the living quarters at the warehouse.

"Huh?" Martin looked up from the table where he was sitting and talking with Boaz. "What are you talking about?"

"We need to go to New Bern. I've got a letter from your cousin that he's asked me to take to the attorney for that Dudley woman."

"Dudley woman? What Dudley woman?" asked Martin.

"She's the woman who was robbed, whose husband was killed," Adam answered.

"How'd you learn her name?" asked Boaz. "Even Lawson hadn't been told who she was."

"Will learned who she was from a colleague. Those who know

her have wanted to keep her name out of the papers, though, for the woman's safety, since those highwaymen still haven't been caught."

"So what's this letter about that Will wants us to deliver?" asked Martin.

"I'm getting to that," said Adam. He crossed over and pulled up a chair at the table to sit down with them. "Guess what the woman's first name is."

Boaz shrugged and shook his head. "No idea."

"Just tell us," said Martin, increasingly irritated.

"Hyacinth. Her name is Hyacinth."

Boaz's eyes grew large. "Oh really?"

Adam nodded. "Yep."

"What's that got to do with anything?" said Martin.

"Don't you remember?" said Adam. "The silver mirror that corpse had in his pocket—it had a hyacinth blossom on it."

Martin's eyes also grew large and he slapped his leg. "I'll be damned! You're right!"

"Well, you know more than me," said Boaz. "I talked to Lawson, and he's going up to Harlowe Creek tomorrow with a couple of men to see that corpse for himself, but I was going to ask you to go with him. I reckon if you need to go to New Bern, though, I can just send Jones with him."

Martin rolled his eyes, then looked at Adam and chuckled. "Oh, Jones'll just love that."

"I don't care if he loves it or not," said Boaz. "Only three of y'all who went out there yesterday are still in town. That Ben fella has taken off, and somebody needs to show Lawson and his men where that body is."

"Did he have any ideas about Ed Willis?" Adam asked.

Boaz shook his head. "Unfortunately, no, but he did say that he'd probably be able to guess at how long that body's been in the creek when he sees it. He also said that depending on how damaged the body is, even though he won't be able to tell for sure, he ought to at least be able to rule in or rule out whether or not the knife that killed that man up at Harlowe Creek could be the same kind that killed Ed Willis."

"How in the world is he gonna do that?" asked Martin.

Boaz shrugged. "Don't know exactly. He said somehow they'd be able to look at the size of the wound and that would tell them whether they were at least made by similar-type weapons."

"Does he think it's likely that both men were killed by the same person?" Adam asked.

"He thinks they were," said Boaz, "but not because of any evidence he has—says it's just a feeling in his gut. It ain't like we're livin in some big city where there's a bunch of crime. You get two stabbins and they happen ten miles apart—first stabbins we've even seen around these parts in I don't know how many years— what are the chances that they're unrelated?"

"That's true," said Martin.

"Mm-hmm. Makes sense to me, too," Adam agreed.

"And I gotta tell y'all somethin else," said Boaz. "It's real interestin about that woman up in Craven County bein named Hyacinth Dudley and that flower on the mirror was a hyacinth. Lawson said he has a feelin that the corpse up in the marsh was either robbed by those same bandits, or he might even be one of those bandits. Said it would make sense to him."

"Interesting," said Adam. "It wouldn't surprise me, but what made him say that?"

"The way Lawson figures it, that woman and her husband were attacked a couple of weeks ago. If those men were headed south rather than north, then they'd have passed right through here. That Dudley man got killed while they were robbin him and his wife. So it sounds like they started out as thieves, not killers. Looks like Ed Willis was also killed for money. Y'all said that corpse had nothing on him except the mirror you found and the canteen nearby. It don't make sense that someone would be just wandering through the swamp with empty pockets and nothin on him. Now they might've come across another traveler and robbed him blind and killed him—and that could be who you found—or they coulda got into a fight somewhere along the way and one of 'em killed the other one."

"Why do you figure whoever killed that man in the swamp didn't take the mirror, too, then?" asked Adam.

"Don't ask me," said Boaz. "Mighta just been a careless mistake."

"So when do you want to leave for New Bern?" Martin asked Adam.

"First thing in the morning, I reckon."

"It's gonna be damned cold out on the water, you know that," Martin said.

Adam nodded. "Yes, it will, but would you rather deal with cold weather or cold-blooded murderers?"

"Fair enough," said Martin.

Chapter Twenty-Two

ADAM AND MARTIN ULTIMATELY AGREED to leave at dawn. In fact, Martin and Jones both came and stayed in the living quarters at the warehouse the night before so they'd all be ready to go at first light.

Emmanuel was so happy to have them all there and safe in his warehouse that he got out of bed to visit with them all. Boaz and Adam informed him of everything they had learned while he had been out of commission. He was relieved to know that investigations were underway and that there may be helpful clues overlapping between the cases.

He also was happy to have all of "his boys" there so they could spend a bit of time together remembering their friend Ed Willis. It was only too bad that Elliot and Joe weren't around as well.

"Another thing's sure," said Emmanuel. "You all will be quite safe here together. I dare any madman to try and do violence against this sturdy crew."

After a night of reminiscing about Ed Willis and formulating ideas about how the perpetrators might be apprehended, they turned in early so those who would be traveling could get an early start. Martin and Jones slept on quilt pallets in the sitting room, while Emmanuel, Boaz, and Adam all slept in their own rooms.

The next morning, when Emmanuel gave the wake-up call, Adam wasted no time climbing out of bed and getting ready to make the trip to New Bern with Martin.

Boaz had made a pot of coffee and fried up a mess of bacon and eggs in the big dutch oven—enough for everybody to have a good breakfast before going their separate ways.

Jones took off to meet the constable down near the magistrate's office, which was very near the Topsail Tavern.

Adam and Martin had a much longer trip ahead of them, so after getting their provisions ready to go, they put on wool hats, gloves, and several layers of clothing. Just before they left, Emmanuel pulled Adam aside and gave him a hand-stitched men's pocketbook that featured a colorful design of a ship at sea. It was shaped like an envelope and had two pockets inside—an empty one for special papers, and another in which Emmanuel had put several dollars for Adam to use to fund the journey. "E. Rogers" was embroidered on the flap.

"Be careful with this. Your grandmother made it for me when we were very young," he said.

Adam looked at the gift in amazement. "Thank you. I certainly will."

After that he and Martin were soon making their way north via the frigid waters of Taylor Creek.

Oh, this was so much easier when we traveled a couple of weeks ago, thought Adam. *We'll be blocks of ice by the time we get to New Bern.*

Neither of them said much until they were nearing Core Banks. They would be sailing via the same route they had taken before.

As THEY NEARED CEDAR ISLAND, which was just a little ways across the water from Portsmouth Island, they couldn't help but think about Ed Willis's family and wonder out loud about how they had taken the news of his murder. He didn't have much family living—just his father and stepmother and some much younger half siblings, whom he barely knew. Adam remembered Ed telling him that he had left home when he was very young because his mother had died and his father was a terrible drunk. And as was always the case in Emmanuel's company, Ed had a family connection to someone Emmanuel knew from his time sailing with Blackbeard. In this case, Ed's mother was the sister of one of Emmanuel's old friends in the notorious pirate's crew.

Adam always wondered what it was about that period of his grandfather's life that made Emmanuel feel such a kinship with all of the men he knew then. Granted, most of them had been from Bath Town, and they had certainly shared harrowing experiences. Then again, thinking about it that way, maybe Adam understood more than he realized. After all that had happened to him since he began his apprenticeship, he certainly felt a kinship with the men in Rogers's Shipping Company. He couldn't imagine a time in his life when he wouldn't see them all as one big family.

And that was actually starting to worry him about Martin. Other than the few words they'd exchanged near Harker's Island

and their brief conversation about Ed Willis's family, Martin had barely spoken. His behavior was getting stranger and stranger—first being so short-tempered, then engaging in increasingly risky and reckless behaviors, and now seeming so completely withdrawn. No doubt about it—Martin was hiding some kind of secret, and Adam had no idea what it was.

"I wonder how Aunt Celie and Annabelle are getting along," Adam said, attempting to make conversation.

"Annabelle?" Martin gave him a confused look.

"You remember. Charles Jr.'s betrothed."

Martin looked like he was thinking for a moment, though Adam couldn't be sure he was considering the topic at hand, then finally said, "I don't know. I reckon if they ain't gettin along we'll just bring Aunt Celie back to Beaufort with us."

Adam nodded. "Yeah. That's exactly what your cousin said we should do. Don't know that she'd want to come back with just us, though. That old woman seemed real nervous to make the trip last time, and Laney was with her."

"Maybe," said Martin.

Maybe? Maybe what? Adam wondered if Martin was even paying attention to the conversation.

"Here, take this for a minute," Martin said, motioning to the tiller.

Adam got up from his place tending the sheets and stepped to the rear of the vessel and took the helm.

Martin moved a few feet away and leaned against the gunwale and unfastened his breeches.

That was nothing unusual. The call of nature didn't wait until one was back on dry land. In fact, when they had made the trip a couple of weeks prior with Laney and Aunt Celie, when the women had to relieve themselves they were able to make use of a chamber pot for that very purpose and then empty its contents overboard.

Now that it was just Adam and Martin, there was no need for either of them to stand on ceremony to do their business.

Still, after a couple of minutes it dawned on Adam that it was taking Martin longer than it normally would to conduct such a *transaction*, so he decided to ask what was taking him so long.

"You alright?"

It took a couple of seconds, but Martin responded, "I'm tryin to piss. Is that alright with you?"

"It shouldn't be that difficult," said Adam. "Maybe if you stop playing with it…"

He looked up and saw that Martin was leaning forward and holding on to the lower shroud. His body seemed stiff, and his face was as white as a sheet.

"You sure you're alright?"

Martin hunched over. Adam lashed the tiller in place and went over to see if his friend needed help.

"Get away!" Martin demanded.

Adam could see that Martin was in pain, and he was at a loss as to what he should do.

"You're not well," said Adam. "How can I help you? Tell me what I should do."

"Just go back to the tiller and make sure we don't run aground!"

Adam started to go back to the helm, but after taking a couple of steps he turned and looked back at Martin. Martin had collapsed on a bench near where he had been standing. He was hunched over in pain. Adam knew there was nothing he could do for him, but he also worried they might not make it all the way to New Bern with Martin in the condition he was in.

He didn't say anything right away, but after a couple of minutes he said, "What is it?"

Martin had his elbows on his knees and was resting his head on his hands. He shook his head.

"Come on," said Adam. "You've got to have some idea of what's wrong with you. It's not supposed to be that hard to take a piss."

Martin chuckled like he was annoyed. "What do you know?"

"I know it's not that hard to take a piss, just like I said—unless something is *really* wrong. I can see that you're in pain. So what is it?"

Martin looked up. "I don't know? Maybe I'm dyin."

Adam scoffed. "I doubt that, but something's definitely wrong with you."

Martin looked out onto the water, seemingly unwilling to make eye contact with Adam. "You just keep behaving yourself and you'll be fine."

"What's that supposed to mean?" asked Adam.

Martin seemed to be thinking about what to say. "You ever heard the saying 'A night with Venus, a lifetime with mercury'?"

"Huh?" Adam wrinkled his brow. After a few seconds he reacted. "Oh... OH! Wait just a minute!... You think you have *the pox*?" His eyes grew wide.

Martin turned back and looked at Adam, but he said nothing.

"Since when?... From who?"

Martin tipped his head to the side and rolled his eyes at Adam. "How in the hell am I supposed to know that? Do you think I would have knowingly taken a turn with a poxy wench?"

Adam gave him a half smile and shrugged. "Don't know. You might. If she's got a pretty face and she's willing."

Martin was clearly not amused.

"When did you first start… noticing a problem?" Adam asked.

"Ugh!" Martin growled. "Why are there always so many damned questions with you? I'm not gonna talk about it. Now get over here and you tend the sheets. I'll manage the helm."

Adam stood and carefully moved back towards the mast to change places with Martin.

For the rest of the evening until the next morning, the two of them barely spoke, except for what was absolutely necessary to either handle the vessel or to share some of the provisions they had brought.

The whole situation was disheartening to Adam. He looked at Martin like a big brother. He had taken him under his wing at Roger's Shipping Company from the very start, which especially helped when Boaz was being his typical grouchy self. For Martin to have changed so much, and for him to be so seemingly incapable of understanding Adam's concern in the situation, was troubling.

Adam understood there was nothing he could do, but at the very least he knew that if Martin didn't get help for whatever condition he had, he was only going to get worse.

FORTUNATELY, THANKS TO WINDS FROM the south, they were able to make good time and rounded Cedar Island before sundown. They had a smooth journey up the Neuse River overnight and made it to New Bern early the following afternoon. That meant they still had time to find Will's attorney friend before nightfall.

A problem arose, however, when it became apparent that

Martin's condition was worsening. As soon as they docked, Adam insisted on finding him a physician.

When Adam asked a man who was doing repairs on one of the docks at the wharf, he learned there was a doctor on the next block. He then asked Martin if he wanted him to hire a driver, but he said he thought he could make it on foot.

When they finally arrived at the address they had been given for the physician, Adam approached the front door, but Martin was having second thoughts.

"I don't know that this is such a good idea," he said.

"What's wrong with it? The place looks good. He's obviously doing well in his business."

Martin winced. Adam suspected his friend was nervous at the sight of the doctor's residence. It was a fine home, so the doctor was presumably a gentleman. Adam reckoned that it was embarrassing to his friend because of the particular condition for which he was seeking treatment.

Adam rapped on the front door. There was no answer, but he could hear noise coming from inside.

"Come on," said Martin. "Let's just go."

Adam said, "Go where? Somebody's here. I can hear them inside. Maybe it's just taking him a little while to get to the—"

Just then the front door swung open, and there was a man standing there who looked like he might be in his sixties. He was of average height and had wispy gray hair on the sides of his head but was mostly bald on top. The hair he did have he kept pulled back in a ribbon. He also wore a pair of thick glasses.

"Good afternoon, sir," said Adam. "Are you Dr. Beasley?"

The man nodded. "I am. How may I be of assistance to you?"

"My friend here"—Adam motioned down the steps to

Martin—"he's not well. We were hoping you might be able to help him."

The doctor peered over his glasses at Martin. "Hmm. I see." He waved the two of them inside.

Once they were all standing in the foyer, Dr. Beasley asked Martin, "What sort of trouble are you having, young man?"

Martin looked embarrassed. "Well, sir, I don't quite know how to…" He looked over in Adam's direction as though he was embarrassed.

Dr. Beasley nodded. "I see. Why don't you come with me then, young man?"

He suggested Adam have a seat while he took Martin to his examination room.

Martin followed the doctor down a short hallway, and Adam waited in an armchair in the parlor. He noticed that the whole house appeared to be wallpapered with the most unusual assortment of patterns from room to room, but they all looked fancy. It was as if the old man was shown all the varieties of wallpaper that were available to him and decided to have a room done in each.

After about five minutes Dr. Beasley came out and told Adam that he was doing a test with Martin and that it might be an hour or so before he was done, depending on the severity of his condition. He told Adam he could continue to wait in the parlor if he wanted to, or he could come back in a couple of hours.

"What is it?" Adam asked. "The test, I mean."

"Oh," said the doctor, "indeed. Mr. Smith claims he has avoided drinking any liquids since last evening for fear of another painful episode. However, I need to reproduce his symptoms so that I can better ascertain what is wrong with him. He is presently drinking a large jug of cool water. Depending on how long it takes for that to find its way to his bladder, we may be done sooner or later."

"I see," said Adam. "Well, if it'll be a while, maybe I should go take care of another matter of business and then come back."

"That'll be fine," said Dr. Beasley.

WHILE MARTIN WAS WITH THE doctor, Adam decided to go to the Martin estate, which was just two blocks to the west, to let Charles Jr. know that he and Martin were in town. He wanted to avoid them just popping up on the doorstep after dark, especially considering the circumstances under which the master of the property had evacuated the town with his own family.

Adam was relieved to find Charles Jr. working outside. He explained to him what had brought them to town and said that Martin was taking care of some business elsewhere but would be returning with him shortly. Then he asked to borrow the mule cart to go see Will's attorney friend and then bring Martin back to the estate.

Within a few minutes he had found the home of the attorney for Mrs. Dudley, Alexander Pearce. He knocked on the door but could tell as soon as he arrived there that it was unlikely anyone was home. No answer. He would have to wait and come back by with Martin later, or else return there the next morning.

There was nothing left to do but go back to Dr. Beasley's place and wait.

Oh please, God, don't let him have the pox, Adam silently prayed as he knocked and stood at the front door until he was invited back in to the doctor's residence. While no one close to him had ever suffered from the pox, he'd certainly heard plenty about it and even seen drawings of the disfigurations the disease could cause. It was not an unusual occurrence, for instance, for a pox sufferer to eventually lose their nose and be forced to wear a false one. Not to mention all of the physical discomfort that such a diagnosis would foretell—much of which came from the treatment itself.

And on a very real level, Adam also wondered what it would mean for him if Martin had the pox. He was fairly certain he understood how the disease was usually acquired—and that part didn't worry him, of course—but he wasn't sure if one could catch it from just casually being around someone, or, for instance, sharing a swig from the same bottle of rum.

There was one thing he did know: Emmanuel would never let Martin hear the end of it if he had gotten the pox. He could just hear it now. Emmanuel would probably say, "You're reaping what you've sown, young man, with all that whoring around!" He often warned the men in his company about just that sort of behavior, telling them that he'd seen with his own two eyes the devastation the pox could cause, as he'd known men who'd had it, and that no fleeting pleasure was worth the high price of such a hellish disease.

Dr. Beasley opened the door and motioned for him to come inside, and Adam saw Martin sitting there in the parlor, waiting.

"You're already done?" he asked as he tried to read the results from his friend's face.

"Well," said Dr. Beasley, "it's a good thing you came back sooner rather than later, but I suppose it's Mr. Smith's place to tell you about his results. I have written him a script for some medicine." He turned to Martin. "You'll need to hurry on down to this address so the apothecary can prepare it for you before it's too late."

Martin nodded. "Will do."

Adam looked at the grandfather clock next to the door and saw that it was already after three o'clock.

"Are you sure the chemist will be there?" he asked.

"I should hope so," said Dr. Beasley. "In any case he lives upstairs, so if he isn't in his shop I'm sure you can find a way to get his attention somehow. Tell him I sent you and that this must be prepared and administered statim."

"What's that mean?" asked Martin.

"Immediately," said Dr. Beasley. "The longer you wait, the worse it will be."

After that, Adam and Martin thanked the doctor for seeing them so late in the day, and Martin paid the man for his service.

When they got outside, Martin saw that Adam had brought the mule, and he patted him on the back and said, "Thank God for beasts of burden, eh?"

Adam gave Martin a strange look. "Sure, I reckon."

He could tell Martin seemed to be in a better mood than when they had arrived.

As soon as they were in the mule cart and on their way to the apothecary one block over, Adam asked him, "How did everything go?"

Martin took a deep breath and sighed. "Well, thank the Lord. He says he don't think I've got what I was *thinkin* I had."

"Hmph. That is good. So what did he say it was?"

"It could still be serious, but he thinks since I'm otherwise healthy, and if I can get that medicine, I ought to be alright. Can't drink nothin stronger than beer for a while, though."

"You still didn't say what it was that you have," said Adam.

"He thinks it's got to do with my bladder. Some kind of urine infection or somethin."

"How does he know it's that and not that other thing?"

"He says there's other symptoms I'd prob'ly have if that's what it was. Course he also said I need to count my lucky stars, 'cause that pox is everywhere."

"You already knew that, Martin," said Adam. "That ain't news."

"I know, but I think this whole experience has taught me at least one thing."

"What's that?"

"I can't tell you. You're too young." Martin laughed.

Adam rolled his eyes. "Oh goodness gracious. You'll never learn, will you?"

Martin shrugged. "Time will tell, won't it?"

"I think this is it," Adam said as he pointed to a building on the corner of Pollock and Middle Streets. "Bradley Apothecary."

As soon as the mule stopped, Martin got out of the cart and checked to see if the door was open. Fortunately, it was. He went inside and came back out a few minutes later with a bottle of dark liquid and a cloth sack with contents that were unknown to Adam.

"What all do you have to take?" he asked.

"This liquid is some kind of cranberry syrup. The man said it was real strong, but that I ought to start noticing some improvement soon, and in here is a mixture of powders and herbs that he's told me to take as a tea."

"That's all? That doesn't sound so bad," said Adam. "At least there's no mercury."

"It's still early enough. I reckon we can run on by and see that attorney friend of Will's," said Martin.

"Are you sure you don't want to just go back to the house and rest this evening? We can go see Mr. Pearce first thing in the morning."

"Nah," said Martin. "Let's just go on and get it out of the way."

Chapter Twenty-Three

"AND YOU'RE SURE IT WAS a hyacinth blossom?" asked Mr. Pearce.

The thirtysomething-year-old lawyer had light-brown hair and hazel eyes, and he was slightly short and stout. He wore a pair of spectacles perched on the end of his nose, giving him an intellectual air. He was the sort of fellow that less educated men would be hesitant to question for fear of being wrong.

"I am, sir," said Adam. "I didn't think it was anything important, but Will—ah, Mr. Martin—he mentioned about your client's name and that the mirror might have something to do with those bandits."

"I should think it very well might," said Mr. Pearce. "Particularly considering the mirror was found in the pocket of the dead man you mentioned. And tell me his initials again."

"RJ," said Adam.

Mr. Pearce dipped his pen in the jar of ink on his desk and scribbled down some notes.

"How long will you fellows be here in New Bern?"

Adam and Martin looked at each other. Martin appeared to defer to Adam for an answer, since Adam's grandfather was the one who'd allowed them to go in the first place.

"Well, sir, I reckon we can stay around another day or two if we need to, but if we're gone much longer than that they may well send a search party for us."

Mr. Pearce nodded. "Certainly. Certainly. I understand. I would like to go and speak with Mrs. Dudley, see what she has to say about the man whose body you saw, the mirror, and the canteen with the initials. Some of it may help her to remember a few more details. I think it would also be a worthwhile exercise to go back and see if there have been any notices about anyone with the initials RJ or anyone who might be missing. Surely that fellow you saw in the marsh has family somewhere. Maybe they're looking for him even now."

Adam nodded. "Maybe so. Where would you recommend we check on that—those notices, I mean?"

"In past issues of the *Gazette*. Go see James Davis. That'd be the best place to start."

As soon as Adam and Martin left Mr. Pearce's office, they went right to James Davis's print shop. Mr. Davis wasn't in, but his apprentice, Thomas, was there.

Adam presented his query regarding the initials RJ. He asked if there had been any notices in the paper in recent weeks, or even months, about anyone with those initials. Thomas said he could thumb through as many issues as they had on hand and look at papers that they had from other colonies as well. Adam and Martin offered to help, and Thomas agreed.

Thomas showed them into the back room, where Mr. Davis kept back issues of all of the papers he had printed. He explained that they were in chronological order in sets of filing cabinets that each had two columns of twelve wide, short drawers, each no deeper than four inches from top to bottom. There were two months' worth of papers in each drawer, starting with January and February in the top drawer, then March and April, and so on. All together there were four years' worth of newspapers in each cabinet. The paper was only printed weekly, so that only added up to eight newspapers per drawer for two months. Each paper consisted of no more than four folded sheets, or eight pages total, so the drawers weren't even packed tight.

They decided to only go through the last six months, which meant each of them could take a drawer and be done in short order. Adam took early December and November, Martin took October and September, and Thomas took July and August.

The job went even quicker than they had expected, considering that most papers were only six or eight pages, and the first four or five were often focused on official public announcements and that sort of news, along with serials. They were able to quickly scan the back pages for any sort of local news.

They mostly just found lots of items about merchant shipments available for sale, rewards for the apprehension of runaway slaves, horses that wandered off, or stolen household items, and of course the occasional stories about local crimes. None of them fit the RJ initials profile until Martin found something from late October. It was a notice from Beaufort County that said:

BATH, October 12.

By an authentic account from Bath, the perpetrator of the horrid murder and robbery committed there sometime ago, as mentioned in this paper, is discovered, and proves to be Mr. Henry Paxon himself, the owner of the store that was robbed, who is now in gaol, and is soon to take his trial for that atrocious crime. Most of the goods were the property of several persons, and were found buried near Mr. Paxon's own carriage house, and the linens and other perishable articles were mostly spoiled. When we consider Mr. Paxon as a gentleman who had long lived at Bath in the character of a worthy member of society, and a man of property, we shall be much at a loss to account for his inducement to murder his storekeeper, and rob the store. Surely something more than avarice must have tempted him to violate the sacred tie of friendship and so daringly offend against his God and his conscience. Although Mr. Paxon has not proven himself to be a reliable witness, in that his schemes have consisted of an elaborate effort to conceal his evil deeds, he has said he had two accomplices, whose role in the plot was to extract the goods from their buried location and sell them south of here for cash in hand. If his tale has any truth to it, certainly only Divine Providence can be credited for causing those men to fail in their appointed task so that Paxon's villainy might be uncovered. If such accomplices do exist, we are told they are brothers called Harmon and Reuben Jones.

"Harmon and Reuben Jones," said Martin. "Rueben Jones, RJ—y'all reckon this might be who we're lookin for?"

"Let me read that," said Adam. He quickly skimmed through the piece of news from Bath and nodded with interest. "Sure seems like it could be. This definitely has to do with a robbery."

"You could find out for sure," said Thomas, "but you'd probably need to go to Bath and talk to that Paxon fellow."

Martin took an exasperated breath. "Bath! There's no way we're goin all the way up there—at least not on this trip. That's a full day's journey from here, and even farther from Beaufort. We need to get back home before we go anywhere else, and it's too cold to be going all over Hell and Creation."

Adam nodded in agreement. "He's right. We're going to have to leave here tomorrow, or the next day at the very latest. Isn't there a post rider or anybody who regularly goes up that way?"

Thomas thought about it for a minute. "You know, there's a county justice by the name of Mr. Bryan from over in Swift Creek. He's here in town a few days at a time near about every week right now, and Swift Creek is less than twenty miles from here and about another twenty miles or so from the Pamlico River. If you can catch him here before he leaves town to go back home tomorrow, you can talk to him and see if he doesn't have anyone he could send to talk to this Mr. Paxon at the gaol there. He might be able to find out by Sunday, then bring word back here when he's back in town next week."

Adam and Martin exchanged glances.

"Sounds like a good plan to me," said Martin. "Where would we find this Justice Bryan now? He's down at the courthouse?"

"He might be," said Thomas, looking at the clock. "Then

again it's getting late. If he's not there, he has a house over on the corner of Johnson and Middle Streets. It's a modest-sized lot with a big, old pecan tree in the front yard."

"Fine," said Adam. "We'll go try to find him now. We appreciate all your help."

"My pleasure," said Thomas. "If there's anything else we can do for you here at the *Gazette*, just stop by."

WHEN THEY LEFT THE NEWSPAPER, Martin admitted to Adam that he was having a lot of discomfort and thought they should go back to the house and wait and see Mr. Bryan the next morning. Adam at first suggested Martin go on back to the estate by himself, but then he realized Martin was dependent on his help to get him there.

They climbed into the mule cart, and Adam drove them back to the house. Martin went right upstairs and didn't even have supper. Adam made it a point, however, to ensure he had plenty of hot water for making the tea he was supposed to drink, and plenty of beer to keep his kidneys flushed.

Chapter Twenty-Four

THE NEXT MORNING ADAM GOT an early start. He wanted to make sure to find Justice Bryan before he returned to Swift Creek.

"'Scuse me, Mr. Adam."

He was startled in the scullery as he kneeled down to move the kettle over the fire to boil water. Aunt Celie was standing behind him, wringing her hands nervously in front of her apron.

"Aunt Celie," said Adam as he stood and turned around to face her. "Are you doing alright this morning?"

"Well, sir, I just as soon you'd take me back with y'all when you go home tomorra, if that's alright."

Though she held a serious face before him now, she looked like she had been crying.

"Of course. That's just fine."

Adam put his hand on her shoulder and motioned that she could have a seat with him at the butcher block table in the center of the room if she wanted. It was something he thought nothing of doing, but he could immediately tell Aunt Celie was unaccustomed to such an invitation. He proceeded to tear a piece of bread off of the loaf in front of him and slather it generously with butter, then took a bite.

Aunt Celie would not sit down. "What time'll y'all be leavin, so I can have my things ready?"

Adam finished chewing. "I reckon we'll leave as soon as the sun comes up. Are you sure you don't want to stay here with Charles Jr.? It's not like you get to see him all the time."

The old woman shook her head. "Naw. I don't 'spect he really even wantin me here, with that young girl of his and all. I reckon I jess in the way."

"Won't you sit down with me?" said Adam. "I'd rather not have to eat alone."

She seemed uneasy about it, and Adam could tell.

"It's alright, Aunt Celie. Nobody's here but you and me. Martin's dead to the world upstairs right now."

Finally, she pulled the chair out and sat down in the chair beside him.

"Want me to fix you somethin else to eat, Mr. Adam?" she asked.

He shook his head. "No, this bread is so good. You made this, didn't you?"

She nodded.

"I can tell," he said. "I don't know anybody who can fix bread like this. It's so light and airy on the inside, but the outside is so nice and crisp."

Aunt Celie looked down at the floor, but Adam could see she had a little smile on her face.

"Tell me something," he said to her. "What makes you think Charles Jr. doesn't want you here just because of Annabelle?"

The old woman was pensive. Adam knew she was reluctant to engage in conversation with him. Still, he was determined to get her to talk. He thought all of this protocol was foolish, especially with nobody else around to see them sitting at the table together.

"I'm asking you," said Adam, "because I have a mama, too, and I know if I didn't get to see her that often I'd sure not want her to run off just because I have a young bride or a fiancée."

"Oh, child," she said, "things's diff'rent with us and with y'all. Things even mo diff'rent with Charles Jr. and me."

"Why do you say that?" Adam asked.

"Well"—she thought for a moment—"'cause he wantin to be free, but you see, I know, I *know* freedom ain't gon' be nothin in the world but a whole mess a trouble. He don't wanna belong to nobody—not even good white folks like these Martins. He say he wantin to be his own man. So he ain't gon' belong *nowhere*. And I can't tell him nothin, 'cause he ain't wantin to listen to nothin I say anyway. Ain't no white folks gon' care nothin for him or that haughty yella girl of his like this family here do."

Adam really had no idea what to say to any of that. "I'm a freeman, and I've obviously never been in your situation—as a slave, I mean—but I don't know what that has to do with you being his mama and him being your son. You sure you don't want to stay here at least until after Christmas? Laney's doing just fine, you know."

"What's she eatin?" said Aunt Celie. "'Cause I know that

baby girl sho don't know how to cook. I reckon all them youngins is near 'bout to starve to death, since I ain't there cookin' for 'em."

Adam cocked his head to the side. "Well, she's learning. I had some of her cooking the other day. It wasn't that bad, actually."

Aunt Celie wrinkled her brow in a cross between skepticism and curiosity. "What'd she fix?"

"Grits and bacon."

"Lawd have mercy! She gon' think she really doin somethin now."

"Come on now, Aunt Celie!" Adam smiled broadly. "She knows she'll never be able to cook like you, but she's still trying to learn a few things."

"Hmph." Aunt Celie put her hand over her mouth to cover the fact that she was laughing a little bit.

"Listen," said Adam, "if you really want me and Martin to carry you back to Beaufort, we will, but just give it some thought and talk to Charles Jr. about it first."

"Fine," she said. She then stood from her chair. "Now you sure I can't get you nothin else to eat, Mr. Adam?"

"No, ma'am," he said. "I actually need to go run down to the courthouse. I've got to see a man about something. Martin isn't feeling well, but if he comes downstairs, will you let him know I'll be back directly?"

"Yessir, I will," she said, then disappeared into the kitchen.

Chapter Twenty-Five

WHEN ADAM ARRIVED AT THE courthouse, he saw things exactly as they had been every other time he had been in town—under construction. It seemed efforts to build a new and improved courthouse and prison were never-ending in the capital city, and Adam couldn't help but wonder what was taking them so long to finish the job. Nevertheless, justices held court in the building in spite of its unfinished state, as it was preferable to the private homes or taverns they had been forced to conduct official business in for many years prior.

It turned out to be easier than he had expected to track down Mr. Bryan. The justice was in his chambers, reading over some papers, when Adam arrived. Adam wasted no time explaining the purpose of his visit, including all of the information that he had learned in recent days and his hope that the justice would assist them in seeking information from the prisoner in Bath.

"It's a good thing you came when you did," said Justice Bryan. "I'll be leaving here to go back home to Swift Creek within the hour."

"Do you think you'll be able to get these answers from Mr. Paxon before you come back to New Bern next week?" Adam asked.

"I'll certainly try, but of course it will depend entirely on the weather."

"I understand."

"You know, young man, you and your friend might as well sail directly to Bath. You can easily be there by tomorrow morning if you leave now."

Adam considered what he said.

"It'll only add one more day to your trip. In fact, it probably would take you fellows the same amount of time to get from Bath to Beaufort as it would from New Bern."

"Hmm… Really?" Adam wrinkled his brow. "That's not too bad, then. For some reason, I thought Bath was right much farther from Beaufort than New Bern is."

Justice Bryan nodded. "No, sir. It may even be a tiny bit closer. Still, if you're going to do that, y'all need to get on out of here. Otherwise, you won't make it to the Pamlico Sound before dark."

Adam pulled out his pocket watch and looked at the time. It was nine o'clock. He needed to make a decision, and fast. He didn't want to send Justice Bryan home thinking he needed to have a man go out to Bath to talk to this Paxon fellow, but he also wasn't sure what Martin would say about going straight to Bath. He decided they'd have to risk it. He would go back to the estate and let Martin know that they would have to go to Bath, no arguments. He'd let Aunt Celie know where they were going, so if she wanted a ride back to Beaufort with them, she'd have to come along, because they certainly wouldn't be going back to New Bern again—at least not on this trip.

He thanked Justice Bryan for his time and bade him farewell, then rushed back to let Martin and Aunt Celie know what the plan would be.

Chapter Twenty-Six

"You must be out of your damned mind," Martin said to Adam when he learned they were going to Bath. "Do you know how far that is?"

Adam nodded. "I do. Justice Bryan said if we leave now we ought to get there by tomorrow morning."

Martin gave Adam a skeptical look, then ran straight upstairs to grab his things. He hollered back down the stairs at Adam, "You better find Aunt Celie and let her know. She's got more to pack than I do."

Adam rolled his eyes. He hadn't even thought about that. Aunt Celie came to New Bern with her big old trunk. Would she really have time to get that packed up quickly so they could leave within the hour?

"Oh, yessir!" Aunt Celie said to Adam. "Jess you gimme ten minutes and I be ready to go."

"Are you sure about this?" Adam asked her. "This will be a longer trip than the last one. We've got to go all the way to Bath first."

"I heard you. I'm tellin you I wanna go there. I was borned there in Bath, and I ain't been back since them Martins got married and moved to Beaufort."

At that she excused herself and went out to Charles Jr.'s cabin to pack her things. Adam could hear her and Charles Jr. fussing with each other from inside the house, but he wasn't about to go out there and get in the middle of it. He knew in spite of what Aunt Celie thought that Charles Jr. would not want his mother to leave, but he also knew that Aunt Celie seemed resolute about going her own way.

AN HOUR LATER CHARLES JR. was taking them all down to the wharf in the mule cart. He helped them load the periauger and hugged his mother.

"You sure you won't stay here?" he asked her.

She stood on her tiptoes and gave her son a kiss on the cheek. "Hush now. Lord willin, I'll see you again another time. Maybe you come see me down in Beaufort if you get those papers."

"I'll do it, Mama," he said, then helped her step down into the vessel. He turned his attention to Adam and Martin. "Y'all please take care of my mama. I don't much like her leavin like this, but ain't nobody can tell her nothin. She gon' do her own thing no matter what anybody say."

"We'll take good care of her," said Adam. "She'll be fine."

"I'll guard her with my own life," said Martin. "Anyhow, Laney'd kill me if anything happened to her."

Adam pulled a letter out of his pocket and handed it to Charles Jr.. "Listen," he said. "I need you to take this letter to Mr. Alexander Pearce. Let him know that we've gone to Bath in search of more answers and that this letter will explain everything."

Charles Jr. nodded. "Will do, sir."

Then he waved and watched them untie from the dock and glide out into the river.

The trip to Bath was long and cold, not to mention a little awkward traveling with Aunt Celie but not Laney. Adam noticed the old woman looked exceedingly tense, so he asked her what was wrong.

"Y'all don't never say no prayers 'less somebody tells you to, do you?"

Adam looked at Martin. Martin rolled his eyes.

"You wanted us to say a prayer for safe sailing, didn't you?" Adam asked.

"Well..." She hesitated a minute. "Don't you reckon you should?"

"You're right," said Adam. "How about if I do it now?"

She tsked, then turned her head away. "That'd be fine. Better late than never."

Adam tried hard not to smile. He didn't know why she hadn't just mentioned it before they left the dock rather than sitting there suffering with worry that they'd have a bad trip if they didn't pray first. He thought about Aunt Franny. She wouldn't hesitate to tell him outright that he needed to pray before making a trip like that. He wished Aunt Celie felt at ease with speaking to him as freely, but he understood why she didn't.

Chapter Twenty-Seven

THEY SAILED STRAIGHT THROUGH THE night and made it to the Pamlico River around three o'clock in the morning. Bath Creek came into view just before the breaking of dawn, and Aunt Celie started to weep.

Adam was the first to notice she was crying. "What's wrong, Aunt Celie?"

She dabbed a handkerchief to her eyes and then wiped her nose. She wrung her hands nervously. Adam was sitting next to the mast, where he had been tending the sheets. Aunt Celie sat on a bench directly across from him, so he reached out his hand and gently patted hers for a second before saying, "Oh, don't cry. What is it?"

Tightly clutching her handkerchief, she said, "I ain't been back here in a many a years."

Adam didn't know what to say, so he just smiled at her and gave her a sympathetic nod.

After a few minutes, as they entered the mouth of Bath Creek she pointed to a clearing of land along a high bluff on the western bank.

"See that big ol' house there?" she said.

Adam nodded.

"That's the first English house my husband ever went in. That's the first place he ever set foot on Carolina soil."

Adam looked over at the impressive estate. "How can you tell?"

"That there used to be the govna's house, but it's changed hands since then."

"That was the governor's house? When was this?"

Aunt Celie thought about it for a moment. "It won't even 1720 yet. I's borned in 1720. I reckon it was 1718—summertime. And they was sixty Negroes they put out on the bank that day."

Adam wrinkled his brow in surprise. "Hmph. Did they have a slave market there? I don't remember hearing anything about that."

"No, Fletcher," Martin called out from his place at the helm. "I think you said your grandfather told you about this."

Adam's eyes grew wide. "Wait... so this—I mean, Old Charles—was one of *those* slaves?"

He turned and looked back at Aunt Celie, who was gazing wistfully at the shoreline of the old governor's estate.

"Your husband was brought here by Blackbeard? On the sloop *Adventure*?"

Aunt Celie nonchalantly looked at him and said, "Of course,

Mr. Adam. Where else they be gettin slaves at in this place? This just a little ol' town."

Adam shrugged. He looked back at Martin as if to say, *Can you believe this?!*

Once they came alongside the little town and docked, Martin went to the courthouse, which was right on the eastern bank of the creek, to see if anyone was there yet. He and Adam both expressed gratitude that Aunt Celie was with them, as she knew where the major fixtures were in the town.

While he was gone, Adam learned more from Aunt Celie about hers and Old Charles's history in Bath. He learned that Old Charles was only around thirteen years old when his village in Africa was attacked by a neighboring tribe and he was forced into slavery. He spent a few years enslaved by fellow Africans, who passed him and others who were captured with him from one tribal chief to another, before he finally was taken to the west coast and sold to European traders. From there he was taken to the Caribbean, and then the French Guineaman he was confined to, *La Concorde*, was overtaken by the notorious Blackbeard.

The pirate immediately renamed the vessel *Queen Anne's Revenge* and set sail for North Carolina to deliver his treasure of twice-stolen Africans, but before he did he intentionally wrecked the ship to split his company. Then he ended up taking a smaller crew and sixty of the strongest slaves with him on board his other sloop, *Adventure*, and some weeks later they arrived at that very spot that Aunt Celie had pointed out, where Bath Creek met the Pamlico River.

Adam was so riveted listening to Aunt Celie tell all of this history that when Martin finally came back from the courthouse, he had nearly forgotten the reason they were there.

"The clerk was there," said Martin as he approached the boat.

"I explained to him that we're investigating the crimes in Craven and Carteret Counties on behalf of Constable Lawson Squires and Mrs. Dudley's attorney, Mr. Pearce. He said we can talk to the sheriff about questioning the prisoner Paxon, but we'll have to wait a few more minutes, because he's not in yet."

"Did you see a tavern or anything around?" asked Adam.

Martin shook his head. "No, but I can go back and look for one."

"'Scuse me, Mr. Martin," said Aunt Celie, "but they used to be a place further up that street there." She motioned down the eastern bank of Bath Creek from where they were presently docked. "I can't remember they name, but you'll see the place if it's still there. They got a sign in the front."

"Good. I'll be right back then," said Martin.

Adam decided to ask Celie if she had any family still around Bath.

"No, sir," she said. "Least I don't reckon I do. Nobody who'd remember me anyhow. My mama died a long, long time ago, and I ain't never knowed my daddy. I heard he came here on that same ship with my husband, but he won't never no property of the Brights—they the family that Mrs. Alice come from. She's Laney's mama. He musta been slave to another family 'round here, or else he got carried off by his owner, but I never knew him, and my mama never did talk about him."

"Hmph." Adam smiled. "We've got something in common then. My mama never talked about my daddy when I was growing up either. But I finally did meet him, you know."

"Mm-hmm." Aunt Celie nodded deeply. "I done heard somethin 'bout that from Miss Laney."

"Would you like to wait here at the boat while we're up at the gaol?" Adam asked. "I reckon the sun will warm things up a bit. It won't be as cold as it was overnight."

"I can, Mr. Adam," she said, "if you wantin me to."

Adam could see that while she said she would, she seemed very nervous at the prospect.

"Of course you don't *have* to wait here," he said. "What would you rather do?"

Aunt Celie thought for a minute, as if she was deciding whether or not she should say anything at all. Finally, Adam raised his eyebrows as if to say, *Well, what do you want to do?*

She twisted her handkerchief around in her hand. "Well, Mr. Adam, if it's alright with you I'd just as soon go over there to the gaol with y'all and wait up yonder. Prob'ly be safer than just stayin down here by the boat in this town. Ain't nobody but strangers here now."

Adam smiled at her and nodded. "Alright. I understand. That's just fine."

In fact, he did understand. This was exactly the kind of thing Martin had talked about. The fact was Aunt Celie didn't feel safe waiting out at the boat by herself. She didn't know anyone in Bath anymore, and since no one knew her, some unscrupulous person might think he could do her wrong in some way and get away with it. She knew that just by being with Adam and Martin, she had some visible sense of protection and safety. It was, of course, sad that things were like that, but hers was a very realistic fear.

She lowered her eyes and quietly said, "Thank you, sir."

"Of course," said Adam. "As soon as Martin gets back, we'll all walk over there together."

Within a few minutes Martin came back and said there

199

was indeed a tavern further up the main street. They all liked the idea of going there and having something good and warm to eat but also knew they shouldn't go there with Aunt Celie, since they didn't know anyone in Bath and were concerned they could run into some problems. It was decided that since the gaol was closer to where their boat was docked than the tavern, they'd take care of that business first. After that, Adam would go to the tavern to see if he could get them something to eat. Aunt Celie would wait in the courthouse while the two of them went to talk to the prisoner.

The Bath Town gaol was nothing more than a small cabin just a few dozen feet away from the courthouse, which was also a surprisingly small structure. From what Adam could tell, the courthouse and the gaol, as well as the pillory and stocks, were all in terrible disrepair. For that matter the very lot the buildings sat on appeared to be sinking and full of mud for being far too close to the water.

"Goodness gracious," said Adam as they got nearer to the gaol. "I don't even see how they can keep prisoners in that thing. I mean, seems like they could bust right out if they wanted to!"

Martin laughed and nodded in agreement.

Aunt Celie looked terribly apprehensive about the whole situation. Adam knew she was a worrier, but he also knew that they ought to be done with their business quickly and then be on their way.

The sheriff must have heard someone was looking for him, because almost as soon as they got near to the gaol, he crossed the lawn from the courthouse to greet the three of them.

"Good day to ye," he said. "I've been told you're desiring a word with the prisoner Paxon. What cause would you have, if you mind not me asking?"

"It's good to meet you, sir," said Martin. "We believe he may be able to help confirm for us, or rule out, that a body that was recently discovered in our county belongs to one of the men he claims as accomplices."

"Your county? Pray tell, what county would that be?"

"We're from the county of Carteret, Sheriff," said Martin, matching the older man's serious tone.

Adam tried not to laugh. He'd never heard Martin put on such airs before.

"Carteret, ye say?" said the sheriff. "I reckon that's quite a distance from Bath Town. What cause have ye for thinking that the body you've seen has to do with Paxon's villainy?"

Adam couldn't help but be amused at the sheriff's manner of speaking. It wasn't wrong at all, only it was unusually formal— and almost archaic, with the *ye* and the *pray tell* and the *villainy*. He couldn't figure out why the middle-aged lawman chose to talk that way.

After Martin provided a brief explanation of the situation, the sheriff agreed to let them speak to the prisoner.

Adam could see that Aunt Celie seemed a little nervous. "Before we go in the gaol, Sheriff, would you mind if I escort Aunt Celie here to wait over in the courthouse?"

The sheriff seemed surprised at the request, but he consented.

Adam took Aunt Celie over to the courthouse, which was just a few paces away, and told her he'd be back to get her in just a few minutes. She took a seat on a bench just inside and waited for him there.

It so happened that Mr. Paxon was Bath Town's only prisoner—at least he was as soon as the sheriff released a man named Bob Cobb. He was a town indigent who played an old game with the local authorities by getting into some kind of mischief on particularly cold days so that he could spend the night (or several nights) in the town gaol, only to be let out again when they felt he'd served his time.

When the sheriff let them into the gaol, Adam saw the only prisoner sitting on the floor, back to the wall, and his thoughts briefly drifted back to the crude hut he had been held in at Eduardo's compound in Havana.

"Paxon," said the sheriff in a gruff voice, "these men would like to have a word with ye."

The dejected-looking prisoner hardly looked like he could be the architect of a criminal scheme—especially something as elaborate as the one of which he had been accused. He was in his thirties and had a kind-looking face. His light-brown hair was thinning on top, and wispy pieces fell forward in his face from his ponytail. Adam could see that Martin also seemed taken aback by the appearance of this pitiful-looking man. They exchanged similar glances of confusion and surprise.

The sheriff motioned to the door and said, "I will be waiting here. I cannot leave ye alone with the prisoner, but I will not interfere with your investigation."

Adam raised his eyebrows in surprise. "Uh… Well, thank you, sir. This shouldn't take long."

"Mr. Paxon," said Martin, standing a good distance from the man. "Do you mind if we ask you a couple of questions?"

"What do you want with me?" he replied.

He didn't seem angry or nervous or anything. In fact, he was so calm it was a little unsettling.

"You claim you had two accomplices," said Martin. "We think it's possible that—provided your story is true—one of them was killed over by Harlowe Creek. Would you be able to describe those men you claimed were helpin you, or tell us anything about them other than their names?"

"Why should I?" said Paxon, again very calm, very matter-of-fact. "I've told the constable and the sheriff all that I know. I've told that man's family, too. I didn't kill him. Yes, I *did* have a plot to steal the merchandise and money with those other two men, but I would never commit murder."

"If you know one of those other men is responsible for the murder," said Adam, "seems to me you'd want to see them brought in, to see justice done."

"I understand why you might think that, but they aren't what I'd call *trustworthy*." He stared blankly at the wall in front of him. "Those men are liars. In fact, one of them is a cold-blooded murderer." He turned his blank stare to Adam. "And he's going to get away with it."

"It don't have to be that way, though," said Martin. "If we're able to figure out who these fellas are… to figure out if the man we saw is one of them, we can see to it that they're brought to justice."

"That would be a welcome turn of events, but I put no stock in it," said Paxon. He turned his stare back to the wall in front of him. "Don't think I expect either of those men to come back here and clear my name from that murder charge. It's better for them that I'm in here. More likely, they'd come back here and kill me long before they'd ever be caught."

Adam felt a chill go through him as he heard the prisoner's words. He didn't doubt the veracity of what the man had said. What he did question, however, was how anyone could approach being accused of murder, or counting murderers as your accomplices, as though it were an ordinary everyday thing.

"They can come back and kill you anyway, Paxon," said

Adam. "If you at least describe them to us, the authorities will know who they need to be looking for."

"Foolish boy. I already told the authorities. They think Harmon and Rueben are figments of my imagination. They believe I've concocted them to try to 'get off the hook,' they say."

"Fine," said Adam. "You've already told the authorities all about them. You haven't told us. All we are asking is for you to describe them physically and any distinguishing characteristics or traits they might have."

Paxon was quiet for a minute. Adam and Martin exchanged uncomfortable glances. They weren't sure if he was trying to decide on whether to answer them, or whether he had decided to stay altogether silent.

The sheriff could see what was happening and decided to speak up. "Paxon, I tell ye, ye damned crazy devil, that if ye insist on keeping your lips buttoned thus, I'll take these gentlemen away and I'll not come back even to bring ye supper this night. Now speak, damn ye, or I'm of a right mind to wring that neck of yours forthwith."

Adam's eyes grew wide at the sheriff's threat. He looked at Martin. Then they both turned and gave a nod to Paxon to show they agreed with the sheriff.

Paxon calmly took a deep breath. "Very well, then. The men you are looking for are some years apart in age, and they are brothers. They look nothing alike. I wonder if their mother might not have had them by two different men, yet they insist they have the same father. It's of no matter to me either way."

"How old do you reckon they are?" said Martin.

"I should think Harmon, the oldest, is about forty-five, but Reuben, he's likely around thirty years of age."

"And how do they look?" Adam asked.

"The younger one, Reuben, he has light-brown hair, almost golden—real curly—and light-brown eyes. The older one, Harmon, is showing his age. You can see his hair was black once, but it's streaked now with silver. And his eyes are as blue as the sky. The ladies might think he's a handsome fellow, but they don't know his heart is as black as coal."

"And are they tall, short, average?" asked Adam.

"They're both average I'd say, but Harmon is not quite as tall as Reuben."

"Any scars, habits, anything else that you can tell us about them?" asked Martin.

Paxon thought for a moment. "The older brother, Harmon, is a remarkable musician, but I don't suppose that'll help you much in identifying a dead body, and truth be told I also doubt he'd play a tune in the commission of a crime, so no, I don't have anything else useful to tell you about them." He smiled, then folded his hands over the top of his knees, which he had drawn up close to his body.

Adam looked at Martin. He could tell they were both thinking the same thing.

"I have one more question," said Adam. "Do they have any other brothers or sisters?"

Paxon shook his head. "Not that I'm aware of. I've only ever known the two of them and have never heard them tell of any other family."

"Thank you," said Martin.

Paxon bobbed his head in acknowledgement but made no sound to suggest that he was happy to answer their questions.

"Yes," said Adam, "thank you. I believe you've helped us more than you know."

ONCE ADAM, MARTIN, AND THE sheriff were back outside the locked gaol, the sheriff asked them, "I heard ye talking to Paxon there. 'Tis true that he gave ye information that will be of help to ye?"

Martin gave a deep nod. "Oh yes, sir. He did. We believe the younger brother he described could easily be the one we saw in the marsh at Harlowe Creek, and the older one— well, we suspect we might know who he is, too."

"We need to hurry back to Bath," said Adam, "because I'm sure the man we suspect is the one surviving accomplice is now a good ways south of Beaufort, if he's even gone where he said he was going."

"Where might that be?" asked the sheriff.

"He said he had a sister in Charleston, and that he had nieces and nephews there that he was hoping to go see." Adam thought back on what Paxon had told him. "But if he's the same man who Paxon described, and he really has no other brothers or sisters, it's anybody's guess where the man we're thinking of could have gone."

"That's right," said Martin. "So we do need to be going."

"I oughtn't to stand in yer way then, gentlemen," said the sheriff. "Ye go ahead and fetch yer slave wench from the court-house, and we'll see you off."

"One thing, Sheriff," said Adam.

"What would that be, young man?"

"If we're right about the men who were down in our neck of the woods being the same men that Paxon here was talking about, then it may be that he really is innocent of the murder of his storekeeper."

"It may be that what ye say is true," said the sheriff. "Ye

needn't worry. Our gaol ain't crowded, and we'll want to hear what comes of those other men so that we can be sure we hang the right man."

"We'll send word to you as soon as we have more information," said Adam.

"Very well," said the sheriff.

Adam and Martin bade him farewell, then went to get Aunt Celie.

After that, Adam quickly ran down to the tavern and asked if he could order some beef stew, along with something to carry it in. The proprietor was reluctant to sell one of his jars along with the food, but the price Adam offered was too much for him to resist.

"I can't offer you silverware, though," said the wiry old man. "So I reckon you'll be eatin with your fingers."

"I'm sure we have some spoons on the boat," Adam replied with a chuckle. He knew Valentine would probably have said the same thing.

He also bought a hot loaf of bread, just taken from the oven, and some apple tarts, which the man wrapped in an old newspaper.

Adam rejoined Martin and Aunt Celie, who were shivering as they waited in the periauger.

"Let's go," said Martin. "It's still early. We can make good time if we hurry up. The winds are coming from the northwest—that ought to move us right along."

Adam quickly climbed in and untied them from the dock, and they were on their way. It was only ten when they left Bath. If the winds continued to be cooperative and the seas remained calm, they should make it back to Beaufort no later than ten the next morning.

Chapter Twenty-Eight

THE TRIP FROM BATH TO Beaufort was a blessedly uneventful one. The wind and sea seemed to understand that Adam and company were in a hurry to get home, and so they conspired to get them there quickly and easily.

Martin and Adam were able to draw Aunt Celie into conversation like they had on the trip to New Bern—by getting her to talk about when Will and Laney were children and her own history with the family.

Not long after the Rogers's Shipping Company warehouse came into view, Adam could see Emmanuel and Boaz standing out on the dock, apparently anxiously awaiting their arrival. Adam could tell they were surprised at seeing the old slave woman in the boat with them.

As soon as they docked at the warehouse, Emmanuel said,

"Thank God! I thought you'd be back yesterday and was beginning to worry."

"I'm surprised to see you out here," said Adam. "It's freezing cold!"

"Never mind that," said Emmanuel. "I'm happy you're back safe and sound. Let's go inside, where it's warmer."

Once they were all in the building, Adam explained how they ended up having to go to Bath after learning about another crime, and that one of the alleged accomplices had the same initials that were on the canteen found out at Harlowe Creek. He also explained that after talking to the prisoner at Bath, they thought the musician named Ben might be connected to the murder in the marsh, and possibly the others as well.

Emmanuel and Boaz were both stunned at the revelations and wanted more information, but Martin said he ought to take Aunt Celie on home to Laney's estate.

"Certainly," said Emmanuel. "You go ahead. Adam can fill us in on the rest of the details."

Martin borrowed Emmanuel's horse cart to take Aunt Celie home. As soon as they were gone, Adam and the others went upstairs to the warmth of the living quarters and sat around the table. It occurred to Adam that he was happy to see his grandfather was still up and moving around in spite of the bitter temperature.

Boaz asked, "Now what's this you said about that musician?"

Adam explained that he and Martin believed, based on the description they got from Paxon, that Ben may really be the man who had called himself Harmon Jones, and that the corpse in the marsh fit the description of Rueben Jones, his brother, at least as much as a man could after rotting for a week or two out in the elements.

"And who are Harmon and Rueben Jones?" Emmanuel asked.

Adam explained about the Paxon crime at Bath that had been in the paper. He told about how Paxon had claimed two accomplices had helped him, and that their descriptions fit remarkably well with Ben and the man whose body was in the marsh.

"That seems like quite a leap, don't it?" said Boaz. "Y'all assuming that just because the physical descriptions are similar that they're the same men. What would even make you think that? A lot of men might fit the descriptions Paxon gave."

"That's true," said Adam, "but he said the man called Harmon was a remarkable musician, and the description he gave fit him perfectly. And then Ben goes and disappears the day after we get back from Harlowe Creek. In addition, don't you think it's a little strange that Ben told me his name was Benajah Harmon, but Paxon knew the two brothers as Harmon and Reuben Jones?"

"He has a point," said Emmanuel, hands folded across the table in front of him.

"Hmph." Boaz grunted. "I don't even want to think we invited a killer into our midst at that pig pickin."

"Me neither," said Adam, "but it doesn't really matter what we want to be true."

"Indeed," said Emmanuel. "I would say the most important thing right now is for you to figure out where Ben has gone. You need to hurry down to the Topsail and see what you can find out."

"Wait," said Boaz. "Do you think those other two musicians are also his accomplices?"

Adam shook his head. "I don't think so. The night I first met Ben and Toby, they said they hadn't played together long at all. Only I didn't realize that actually meant they'd only been playing together a few days. When I went by to find Ben on Tuesday morning, James said he had no idea where he'd gone."

"Fine then," said Emmanuel. "I think you ought to go on down to the tavern. Only Martin has just taken the horse cart."

"That's no bother," said Adam. "It'll feel good to walk after so much time the last couple of days on the water."

WHEN HE GOT BACK TO the tavern, he was relieved to find Toby was there.

"I'm glad you stopped by," said the tall red-haired fiddler. "I heard you came here the other day looking for Ben."

"I did," said Adam. "Have you seen him?"

Toby shook his head. "No, I sure haven't, but he left something for you." He went into the room and rifled around through his bag, then brought what looked like the missing journal over to Adam. "James didn't know that Ben had given it to me with the clear instructions to give it to you when I saw you."

Adam took the journal and flipped through the pages to see the notes inside. Everything looked in order.

Toby continued: "I asked Mr. Hodges when you might be back, and he said he wasn't sure, that you'd gone out of town."

Adam nodded. "I did go out of town. Just got back a little while ago. Listen, did Ben happen to leave anything else here, like maybe a silver pocket mirror or something like that?"

Toby laughed. "No, as hard up for money as Ben was, I reckon if he had a silver mirror he likely sold it and used the money to help pay his way down to Charleston. He's a clever rascal."

Oh, thought Adam, *you have no idea.*

He thanked Toby for his time and told him if he heard

SARA WHITFORD

anything from or about Ben to please either let Valentine know, or send word down to Rogers's Shipping Company.

212

Chapter Twenty-Nine

A S SOON AS ADAM LEFT the tavern, he knew his next stop would have to be the only place in town where he knew the owner regularly bought used items off of folks to resell.

Simon Moore, the heir apparent of Moore's Mercantile, was a bright-eyed, amiable, energetic young man who couldn't have been more than thirty-five. His father ran the store before him, but he was now sickly and confined to his bed and was being cared for by Simon's wife and daughter while Simon worked each day.

Before Adam had been apprenticed to Emmanuel, he always loved visiting Moore's shop. He had the best general store in the region, with all sorts of diverse merchandise. Nowadays, though, Adam didn't stop in nearly as often unless he was there conducting business for Emmanuel. Nearly all of the imported goods that were sold at Moore's came into Beaufort through Rogers's Shipping Company.

Today Adam was there on a different kind of business, yet Simon Moore was as friendly and helpful as he'd always been.

"I've seen the fellow you mentioned. He's been in a few times since he came to town. First time he came he wanted to sell a gold locket—very fine piece, but with a broken clasp—and for a reasonable price, too." Simon gave him a sly but friendly smile. "I ought to be able to make a nice profit on it as soon as I get the piece to fix it. Care to see it?"

Adam nodded. "Oh yes, I would."

Simon went to a wooden drawer in the cabinet that was built into the wall behind his counter, and he unlocked it with a key that he kept on a cord around his neck. He pulled a long gold chain out of the drawer with a heavy locket that dangled from it. Adam had a sinking feeling in his stomach as he briefly remembered sitting for Ed Willis on board the *Gypsy* while he painted a tiny portrait of him to go into a locket he'd bought for his mother in Havana.

He hadn't thought about that until just now.

"Here it is," said Simon as he laid the chain and locket out on a piece of soft cloth on the counter. "It's beautiful, isn't it?"

Adam nodded as he closely examined the piece. "Do you mind if I open it?"

"No, of course not. Go right ahead."

Adam carefully picked up the locket and was impressed by its weight. "This must've cost you a great deal of money."

Simon tipped his head to the side and nodded. "Yes, but not nearly as much as he could've gotten for it if he'd have shopped it around. I could tell he was trying to get it out of his hands, though. He said as a musician, never knowing where he was going to stay from town to town, things that valuable could easily be stolen."

"Did he say where it came from?" asked Adam. "I mean, I'm just thinking this must not be a family heirloom or anything for him to part with it so easily."

"No, in fact he said it was actually something another man gave to him as a payment for some money he owed him. Apparently, this little trinket has changed hands more than once."

Adam turned it over, carefully studying both sides as well as the inside—which was empty. There was no hyacinth blossom on it like there had been on the mirror, so nothing about it made it seem like it belonged to Mrs. Dudley. The locket was pretty, but it was very simply engraved, not at all ornate. The greater part of its value was surely in its gold weight.

"I reckon he used part of the money he got for this to pay for his room at the tavern," said Adam.

"Maybe," said Simon. "I know he turned right around and gave me part of the money to buy that guitar he played while he was here. He's already traded it back to me, though, just before he left town. It's right over there." He pointed to a far corner of the mercantile near the store room.

Adam hadn't noticed it before because of all of the bins and shelves and baskets of this and that, but sure enough, there was Ben's guitar.

"You're saying he didn't come to town with that instrument?"

Simon shook his head. "No, sir. He reasoned that he'd buy it and use it to make more money. Smart fellow, if you ask me. Always thinking of ways to improve his situation."

Adam nodded in agreement. "It would seem that way, wouldn't it?" He was sickened to think about just how scheming this man named Harmon, alias Ben, was. "How much did you pay him to buy the guitar back?"

"Just four shillings. Can you believe it?"

Adam looked at Simon in utter confusion. "Four shillings? That's all?"

"Yes. He said he didn't want to travel such a distance with an instrument so large—too cumbersome. Said he didn't need much for it, that he'd made right much money here in town. He said he was just grateful that I had been able to help him out while he was here."

"Hmm." Adam was pensive. "What about a pocket mirror? Did he bring anything like that here?"

Simon shook his head. "No, nothing like that. Why do you ask?"

Adam proceeded to fill Simon in on what he suspected was true of his recent customer.

Simon was understandably dismayed.

"I can't believe it," he said. "Here I've been helping finance this fugitive, thinking he was such a nice fellow! You never know who to trust these days."

"Eh, Simon, you can't blame yourself. You didn't know. None of us knew. For goodness' sake, I invited him out with us to Harlowe Creek. We stood there looking at a dead body, which was apparently his own brother, and he took notes about it like he was a complete stranger. It's frightening to think anyone could be so cold and deceptive."

"He sounds like he could be the Devil's own son."

"I won't argue with you there," said Adam.

He thanked Simon for the information and asked him to send word if he heard anything that might help the authorities locate Ben. Simon said he'd keep an ear out.

Now Adam needed to talk to Emmanuel so they could try and figure out how to track down the killer.

Chapter Thirty

O N THE WAY BACK TO the warehouse, Adam thought about the pocket mirror. What reason would Ben have for not getting rid of it before he left? Surely he could have gotten a few shillings for it, anyway. Maybe he knew it would tie him directly to the Dudley attack.

Also, Ben apparently told everyone he was headed to Charleston to see his sister, but what if that was all a lie? Paxon said he didn't know of Ben or Reuben having any other siblings. He may have gone down to Charleston, but for that matter, he could have gone in any direction.

Adam bounded up the stairs two at a time until he got to the living quarters. He quietly crossed the sitting room to the door of his grandfather's room, and he slowly opened it to peek inside.

"I'm awake, boy," said Emmanuel. "I'm just resting—haven't

done much of that the last couple of days." He was curled up on his side under the covers. His back was facing the wall where the fireplace crackled. "Come in and sit down. Tell me what you've learned."

Adam came in and closed the door behind him so that he wouldn't let the warmth of the room out. He crossed over to the bed and sat in the chair that was next to it. "I've just spoken to Simon Moore. He told me that Ben Harmon, or Harmon Jones—whatever his name is—sold him a valuable gold necklace when he first arrived in town. That was nearly three weeks ago. He spent a little bit of the money he got for it to buy a guitar, which he used to play music at the tavern. The day he left town he sold the same guitar back to Simon for four shillings."

"Did he say anything of the mirror?"

Adam shook his head. "I just told you everything he told me."

Emmanuel clutched hard at the pillow beneath his head. "This man has to be found, Adam. He killed Ed Willis, I'm sure of it, and he must be brought to justice. And I think the authorities would like to ask him of other crimes he's committed. There's no telling how many victims are out there longing for justice, not knowing the name of the man who brought them misery."

Adam leaned forward with his elbows resting on his knees, fingers interwoven. "Don't you worry. We'll find out where he went. I'll track him down myself if I have to."

"Go ask around down by the boats. The fishermen could probably tell you at least if there were any vessels traveling far south from here."

"I'll do it," said Adam.

He stood from the chair and was about to leave the room.

"One thing, though," said Emmanuel.

"What is it?"

"If you learn of his whereabouts, don't be a fool. Do not try to go after this man on your own."

"I promise you I'll come back here for help if I find out where he's gone. Alright?"

Emmanuel gave him a small nod. "Alright. Godspeed."

Chapter Thirty-One

ADAM LEFT THE WAREHOUSE AND went straight down to the town docks, where fishermen were bringing in their catches.

"You sure you haven't seen anyone like him?" Adam asked a couple of men who were bringing in small barrels of fish they had caught.

They shook their heads. One of them said, "We ain't seen nobody 'cept the same ol' rascals out here on the water every day."

The other man said, "Maybe you ought to run over there to Baldwin's place. He's keepin his fingers in everything that's happenin down here."

"I thank you, gentlemen," Adam said, before walking off in the direction of Baldwin's Chandlery.

Faulkner Baldwin had been a merchant like Emmanuel up

until about five years ago. His business had fallen apart after Richard Rasquelle started picking off his customers. Now that Rasquelle was gone, Baldwin had set up shop in the building that had been Rasquelle's warehouse. Baldwin wasn't operating a mercantile business now, though. When he returned to Beaufort, he met with Emmanuel, and the two of them agreed that Beaufort needed a good well-stocked store for ship supplies, so it was decided that Emmanuel would import the goods if Faulkner Baldwin would agree to sell them.

Adam had a burning feeling in the pit of his stomach when he first went through the door on the street side of Baldwin's Ship Chandlery. He remembered the night he had sneaked in there to spy on Rasquelle as though it were yesterday.

The place looked quite a bit different now, though. There were still some barrels along a couple of walls in the place, but now there was a long counter set up at the western end of the building, where Baldwin conducted his sales business.

"Good day, sir," said the short, balding roly-poly man behind the counter. "What might I help you with today?"

Adam crossed the warehouse to where the middle-aged fellow stood and offered to shake his hand. "Hello, sir. My name is Adam Fletcher. I work for Emmanuel Rogers—he's also my grandfather—and I'm afraid I've not had the pleasure of making your acquaintance."

Baldwin enthusiastically shook Adam's hand. "Oh well! Nice to meet you, boy! You're Emmanuel's grandson, you say? I never even knew he had a family."

Adam grinned and nodded but didn't respond to that comment. He hadn't said it to boast about his family relationship to Emmanuel, but rather to establish that he wasn't just some stranger wandering in off the street looking for information.

"Listen, sir," said Adam, "I was told you might be able to help me out with some information. I've been told that you know what's happening down here at the docks better than just about anybody. I was wondering if you knew anything of a man named Ben, or Harmon, who left this town several days ago. He stayed briefly at the Topsail Tavern as a musician, but he left one morning, and no one knows for sure where he's gone."

Baldwin shook his head. "No, I'm afraid I haven't heard of anybody like that."

"It's possible he was using an alias," said Adam. "Have any strangers that you know of hired any captains you know to take them away from here?"

"I can't say that I've heard about any strangers hiring any local captains to take them anywhere. Remember it's winter. Folks aren't much for traveling in this kind of weather."

Adam nodded in agreement. "That's true. This man said he was headed south—to Charleston. Have there even been any ships leaving here that you know of that were headed in that direction, strangers on board or not?"

"Well, let's see here... let me think..." Baldwin leaned forward and rested his chubby elbows on the counter. He ran his finger down some sort of list that was in front of him, then seemed to cross-reference what he had seen there with a calendar he had written out on another paper. "Mm-hmm. Right here, see?" He turned the list and the calendar around and pointed to a date from two weeks earlier. "See, on this day Mr. George Cherry—you know who he is, don't you?—he left with his wife and children to his wife's family's estate in Tortola. There was a death in the family, you know. They went to settle affairs and so Mrs. Cherry can claim her inheritance. I don't reckon they'll be back until spring, or maybe longer."

"And they left two weeks ago?" Adam asked. "Was this common knowledge? I mean, did many folks know about this?"

"Who's to say?" said Baldwin. "I knew about it, but I haven't any idea if he went around telling folks about it."

Adam nodded. "Mr. Cherry doesn't have any slaves, does he? And I don't reckon he'll have any servants staying on the grounds while he's away, will he?"

"Ah, no," said Baldwin. "You know him. He's a Quaker. They don't believe in keeping slaves. But I do know he has a neighbor who was going to check in on his estate from time to time until the Cherrys return—just to make sure everything is in order. You understand?"

"Yes," said Adam. "Well, there's no chance this Ben fellow could've gotten hired to go down to assist the Cherry family on their journey to Tortola. He was still here a week ago."

"That's what I was telling you," said Baldwin. "Other than the regulars going in and out fishing and shrimping and whatnot, there's been no vessel that could've taken this man north, south, or east—at least not leaving from this port. I'd know about it."

"That's fine," said Adam. "Keep your ears open, if you would. Please send word down to us if you hear anything."

"Will do," said Baldwin. "What do y'all want with this fellow anyhow?"

"We believe he killed Ed Willis, and others as well. He's dangerous and should not be given shelter or transportation by anyone for any reason, unless it's in irons and to the gaol."

Chapter Thirty-Two

As soon as Adam left Faulkner Baldwin's Ship Chandlery, he hurried back to the warehouse. He had a sneaking suspicion that Ben, or Harmon—whatever he called himself—was hiding out at George Cherry's estate. He didn't want to go out to the Cherry estate alone, and he had promised Emmanuel he would come back to the warehouse for help if he thought he knew where Harmon was.

Boaz was working down on the floor of the warehouse, shaping staves for casks.

"Martin come back with the horse cart yet?" Adam asked.

"He did. Came back a little while ago, but then he took off again. Said he'd be back later—had some business to tend to."

Adam kicked the ground and stood with his hand on his hip and thought for a moment. "Alright, listen. I think I know where

Harmon's gone off to—and it's not far. I promised Emmanuel I wouldn't go after him by myself, but I think it might be best if I go on out there and check things out. If he's where I think he is and he suspects that anyone knows about it, he won't hang around long."

"Where do you think he's hiding himself?" Boaz put down the stave he was working on and listened attentively for Adam's response.

"Faulkner Baldwin said no ships have gone out of here in the last week. Only thing going in and out of these waters are the local fishermen. He did say that George Cherry and his family left a couple of weeks ago for Tortola, but that was before Harmon left town, so he couldn't have gone with them. If he's heard about them being gone, don't you reckon that would be an ideal place for him to hole up for a while, take some valuables, and maybe even make off with a skiff?"

Boaz considered all that Adam had said. "Well, since you mention it, that sounds just like somethin he'd do. I'll go with you out there. Emmanuel's right—you ought not go after this fella by yourself."

"I think you should stay here with Emmanuel. Just knowing Harmon is still in the area, I'd hesitate to leave him here alone. Emmanuel can barely get around with that arthritis."

"Well, then why don't you just wait until Martin gets here? He can go with you."

"No, daylight's burning. If we wait too long, it'll be dark. I have to go now. You know the Cherry place. It's not far. If there's no evidence of Harmon there, I should be back in under an hour, but if he is there, I'm going to do what I can to keep him from getting away. Just tell Martin as soon as he gets back to meet me at the Cherry estate, and tell him to bring the cart. If things happen the way I expect they will, somebody will likely need to be carried out of there. Lord willing it'll be Harmon and not me."

Chapter Thirty-Three

GEORGE CHERRY'S PLACE WAS LESS than a mile from the warehouse. It was on a creek that flowed out into the North River. It would be an idea place for a criminal to hole up, steal provisions, and possibly even take a skiff and make an escape.

While he was tired from the near-constant traveling, Adam was convinced it was a good idea he was going to the estate on foot rather than horseback. It allowed him to make a much quieter approach and not worry about an animal being spotted out on the lawn if he needed to inconspicuously creep towards the house.

When he arrived on the grounds, it didn't appear to Adam that anyone was there, but then he heard a noise. He quickly ran around the back of the house but didn't see anyone. He checked the outbuildings, but still no one. Then all of a sudden a flash from one of the windows in the residence caught his eye.

He ran towards the house, determined to catch Harmon inside. It frustrated him to know that if Harmon was in there he could just as easily run out the front.

When he got up on the porch to check the back door, he discovered it was unlocked. He opened the door and quietly stepped inside. Not a sound. He tiptoed slowly through the kitchen, then into the dining room. Next he moved through the foyer, then into the parlor and the library, but no one was downstairs.

It was time to go upstairs.

Unfortunately, the third step creaked. He heard movement on the second floor, apparently of Harmon reacting to the sound of him moving through the house. He slowly proceeded up the stairs, which went up straight, then turned left against the opposite wall, then turned left again to enter the second floor.

He was surprised there was no hallway. Instead the second floor entered directly into a little landing area, and there were doors in three directions that were open into the other bedrooms. To the left as he exited the staircase appeared to be the master suite. He peered inside. There was a side room with a writing desk. Just beyond that there was the master bedchamber. He stepped back out into the landing at the top of the stairs. Across the way there was what appeared to be a little girl's room.

He decided to go back through the master suite first. He proceeded through that room and around into the next, which turned out to be what looked like a lady's dressing room. The next room appeared to be some kind of sitting room. He then made it all the way around into the enormous little girl's room. The entire second floor was like a big circle.

Where is he? he thought. He didn't see or hear Harmon even once while he was moving through the upstairs. *Maybe he already ran out the front of the house.*

He went to the windows in the little girl's room that looked out over the front lawn, but the drapes were too swoopy for him to get a good view. He pulled back one of the heavy curtains, then looked closely at everything he could see outside. He thought he saw a figure running in the distance. He squinted his eyes to get a better look.

Just then something grazed past him.

He quickly turned in the direction from which the object came, and he saw Harmon standing in the second-floor entryway. Adam turned to look behind him and saw a knife stuck into the wall from where he had thrown it.

Adam ran over and grabbed the knife, but when he turned to look back where Harmon had been, he wasn't there anymore.

At least he had Harmon's knife now. He looked at the ivory handle, then the blade, and he wondered if this was the knife that was used to kill Ed Willis.

He wanted to run him down now more than ever, but the house was like a maze. He could chase him around and around and never corner him, unless he was careful.

He stood in an alcove next to the stairs in the little second-floor entryway. He decided he wouldn't move, he wouldn't make another sound until he heard Harmon make a noise first.

Sure enough, within a few seconds he heard something coming from the master suite. He glanced around the corner into the room just long enough to get a look at the layout and formulate a plan.

He knew he better do this right. If anything went wrong, Harmon would slip away, and it would be unlikely he could corner him again.

Fortunately, the doors leading into and out of the master suite were both along the same wall. The placement of furniture inside the rooms would prove useful. He'd have to be quick and coordinated to block off *both* doors of the master suite and trap Harmon inside.

His goal wasn't to completely stop Harmon from being able to exit the room. All he needed to do was slow him down enough that he wouldn't be able to get away.

There was a low dresser on the same wall as the two doors leading into and out of the room. Even though it did have a mirror attached, he didn't reckon it would be too heavy to move quickly. There was also a desk and chair just inside the door leading into the master suite from the entryway. He had a plan.

God help me! Adam thought as he quickly ran into master suite and slammed the door behind him. He had no idea where his quarry was hiding, but it was no matter. He intentionally knocked the chair over in front of the door, then ran straight down that same wall and shoved the dresser in front of the other door. He had effectively trapped Harmon inside the master suite with him. He felt confident that he could move faster than the killer, and the adrenaline coursing through his body told him failure was not an option.

He stood along the wall where the dresser had been and watched for him to come out. He didn't have to wait long. Harmon quickly emerged from behind a changing screen and slowly walked towards Adam.

Adam's jaw was tense, and his eyes were narrowed in anger. His heart was racing, but he wasn't intimidated—not even a little bit. He knew Harmon was dangerous, but he also knew he'd caught his other victims off guard. They hadn't been anticipating him trying to kill them. Adam, on the other hand, was ready.

"Whatcha doin boy?" Harmon asked.

Adam said nothing. He only glared at the murderer standing less than twenty feet in front of him.

Harmon started to walk closer. Adam didn't move a muscle.

"What brings you out here, Adam? I ain't got a quarrel with you, you know." He took a few steps closer. "You can just go on your way. We can just both go our own way. I've got a sister waiting to see me in Charleston, but I told you I can't go down there empty-handed. This fella here with this big ol' house"—he motioned around the room—"he's got far more than he needs, don't he? He won't miss it if I just take a few little things." Harmon stuck his hand in his pocket and pulled out some jeweled trinkets he'd picked up around the house and showed them to Adam. "This is all I want right here. See? I reckon them people who live here won't even miss 'em, they've got so many pretty things."

Adam still didn't speak. He only sighed and raised an eyebrow in disbelief. After a second or two he slowly cocked his head to size up his opponent, just like he would in a game of chess. Harmon was about his height. He looked strong, but no more so than any of the men Adam worked with every day. He also knew for a fact that a man Harmon's size, and especially his age, had never been able to take him down at the tavern.

Adam was finding the longer he stayed still and quiet, the more unsettled Harmon appeared to become. The killer was getting fidgety. He seemed nervous. Nervous people did desperate things.

Adam was trying to calculate all of the various moves Harmon could make, given where both of them were standing. He was also calculating what his own response would be to each of them. When he noticed Harmon glimpse down at his hand, he knew his goal was to get the knife away from him.

Adam had been gripping the knife upside down by its handle, with the blade hidden behind his wrist. He didn't want to make this any bloodier than it had to be, and his bare hands had done a fine job in the past of helping him deal with unsavory characters.

For a fleeting moment he thought of how easy it would be to end Harmon's pathetic life with one well-directed thrust of the blade, but then he thought about Ed Willis. If this knife was the one that killed Ed Willis, there was no way Adam wanted to be the next one to take another man's life with it—at least not if he could help it. Nevertheless, he also knew if it came right down to it, he'd kill Harmon before he let Harmon kill him.

In that second Adam knew exactly what to do. He looked at Harmon, then looked across the room to the far side of the bed, where there was the dressing screen and the chamber pot. He quickly tossed the knife across the room so that it landed between the chamber pot and the screen.

Just as Adam expected, Harmon ran towards the knife, but Adam was quicker. He charged at him like a bull and knocked him back, but Harmon was able to regain his footing by holding on to the footboard of the bed and pivoting. He pulled away and tried to take another step, but he didn't get far.

Adam lunged at him full force from behind.

Once he had him down, Adam threw the weight of his body across Harmon's back and pulled his arm up behind him to force him into submission. Harmon kept fighting, though.

"This is no good, boy," a breathless Harmon said, face to the floor, while struggling to breathe from under Adam's hold. "I don't want to kill you, but I will. I told you I ain't got no quarrel with you."

"You won't kill me. I've got your arse on the floor," Adam

said. They were the first words he'd said to the man since he got into the house. "You killed my friend, you worthless snake."

Harmon laughed and tried to take a really good breath. He then suddenly tried to burst up by twisting from under Adam's hold. Adam wasn't having it, though. He shifted his bodyweight a bit, causing Harmon to think he would be able to break loose. As soon as he'd turned himself all the way around so that he was facing Adam, Adam gave him a sturdy punch, which forced the back of Harmon's head to crash against the bricks of the fireplace.

Almost instantly the killer went limp. He wasn't dead, just knocked out.

At that point the only thing Adam had to do was find something to bind the fugitive. He decided the silk ropes that were used to hold back the curtains should work just fine. He made quick work of hog-tying Harmon, binding his hands and feet behind him.

No sooner had he gotten him tied up when Harmon started to come to. The killer had the nerve to mouth off, but Adam didn't let it rattle him.

"You know that friend of yours," said Harmon, lifting his face from the floor to try and look at Adam. "He never even saw it coming. We was sitting at his table playing cards."

"You be quiet," said Adam. "I don't want to hear another word come out of your mouth."

"See, I figured he had a winning hand, but I don't much like losing."

"And yet look at you there," said Adam. He kneeled down and glared at him. "You're tied up just like a hog waiting for the slaughter. Isn't it funny how quickly your situation can change?"

Harmon let out an ungodly scream, either out of sheer desperation or in an attempt to unnerve Adam.

"You might as well settle down," Adam said.

He got up and walked into the little area with the writing desk. He found a book to read, then brought it and the desk chair into the bedchamber, where he sat with his feet propped up on the hearth to keep an eye on the prisoner.

After about fifteen minutes he was relieved to hear Martin hollering outside. "Fletcher! Hey, Fletcher! You in there?"

Adam went to the window in the upstairs entryway and opened it. He called down to his friend, "Get on up here—use the back door." He motioned around to the other side of the house.

Within a few seconds Martin was in the house and running up the stairs.

"Where are you?" he called out.

"In here," said Adam.

Martin observed the scene. He saw Harmon hog-tied on the floor and Adam sitting in the chair next to him with a book in his hand called *The Bruised Reed*.

"Good God Almighty!" Martin exclaimed. "What did you do?"

"I caught him," said Adam. "Bound him up and got him ready for when you arrived."

"How did you know I would be here?" said Martin.

"Because. I told Boaz if I wasn't back in an hour to send somebody. I knew you'd come. And anyway, if you didn't show up shortly, I'd have just dragged his sorry arse down the stairs and dragged him back to town myself. I'm mad enough I near about believe I could do it."

"Oh well I'm almost sorry I came, then," Martin joked.

Adam put the book back on the shelf and then went over

and motioned for Martin to help him pick up Harmon to bring him down the stairs.

They carried him out of the house, pulled the door to—but couldn't lock it, since Harmon had picked the lock and they had no key—then threw him in the back of the horse cart. They went by Constable Squires's house to let him know they'd gotten the fugitive, then carried him, still bound and tied, to the gaol, where the constable untied him and locked him inside.

After that, Adam and Martin returned to the warehouse with a great sense of relief to bring the news that Adam had caught the killer.

Emmanuel was glad to hear it, and Boaz patted Adam on the back. "Well done, boy. I thought you were a fool for going over there by yourself, but it seems like you handled it all just fine. To be honest, though, I'm surprised you didn't kill Harmon yourself right there."

"I'll tell you," said Adam, "I'm like Emmanuel. I want to see him face justice. If it had come right down to it, I wouldn't have hesitated to do whatever was necessary to defend my life, but he turned out to be easier to disable than I expected. He's really not much of a threat without that knife in his hand."

"Still, it was brave of you to rush in there like that, Fletcher," said Martin. "And I'm sure Mr. Cherry will want to reward you somehow when his family gets back from Tortola."

"Eh, I don't care about any of that." Adam shrugged. "You know, it was bad enough that Harmon was a killer, and that he'd fooled us all, but I don't know if I'd have gone after him like that if he hadn't killed Ed Willis. I'd have probably just left it to the authorities."

"Well, I for one am glad you caught him," said Boaz. "I didn't know you had it in you."

Martin laughed. "That's only because you weren't in Havana."

Boaz rolled his eyes and chuckled. "Oh, sure. I forgot."

"Ed's part of the family here," said Adam. "I just couldn't stand the thought of letting him get away with taking him from us."

And part of the family he was. Adam thought about how much his "family" had grown since he had come on board at Rogers's Shipping Company. Up until the day he first started working in the warehouse, his whole family, his whole world, had been wrapped up in the Topsail Tavern, but now he considered not only his biological relations as his family but all of the men at the shipping company, as well as the Martin family. And he thanked God for them all. He would bring to justice anyone who would do any of them harm, by any means necessary.

Chapter Thirty-Four

IT WAS THE WEEK BEFORE Christmas. Adam and Martin were on their way to Laney Martin's estate for a special dinner. Adam noticed Martin seemed pensive. He realized he hadn't thought much about his friend's *ailment* since they got back from Bath.

"You seem awfully quiet. Everything alright?"

Martin tsked and said, "You and your questions!"

"You're my friend," said Adam. He paused and thought for a moment, then said, "You know, you're like a big brother to me. I just want to know whether or not you're fine."

Martin sighed. "Ah, Fletcher. My physical state? I reckon I'm doing right much better in that respect. It's my mind, though, that's givin me all kinds of trouble."

Adam wrinkled up his face. "How do you mean?"

"Well…" Martin took a deep breath and sighed again. "When you been a certain way for as long as you can remember, well, that's just who you are, ain't it?"

"I reckon so," said Adam. But he really had no idea what Martin was getting at.

"And then something happens and it makes you start won-derin—wonderin if you maybe ought to change, but then you just know deep down that you prob'ly can't. 'Cause in the end it's just who you are."

Adam cocked his eyebrow in skepticism at Martin. "Is this about you thinking that you ought to learn some self-control when it comes to women?"

"Well, see, that's the problem. What I think I might ought to do, and what I think I'm likely to do—well, they're two different things."

"Martin Smith!" Adam exclaimed. "I don't understand you at all. A week ago you were worried you could have the pox. By the grace of God you didn't. Is it really that hard to see this whole situation as a second chance for you to try and straighten yourself out?"

"I know it's a second chance, but I don't know that it mat-ters." He shrugged. "I don't really see myself changing, and to tell you the truth it makes me sad to even think about it."

"I don't know what to tell you then," said Adam, laughing. "Sounds to me like you've resigned yourself to having the self-control of a stray dog."

"Don't pass judgment on me, Fletcher," Martin said. "You ain't never even tasted the fruit, so you don't have the foggiest idea what it would be for me to stop enjoying it. Imagine the finest thing you've ever eaten, then being told you won't be able to have it ever again."

"But nobody's telling you that you can't *ever* have it again." Adam thought about exactly how he would say what it was that he wanted to say. "See, what some men do—in case you haven't heard—is they do have fruit as much as they want, only they only pluck it from their *own* garden. They don't go around eating strange fruit from any old place. Isn't that better, after all? When you have your own garden and your own fruit, you can have it right there and ready for you when you want it. And the other great advantage is you don't have to worry about any other strangers eating your fruit. It's only for you." He grinned at Martin.

Martin wrinkled his brow and looked at Adam. "For someone who's never even *had* fruit before, it sure does seem like you've given right much thought to having your own garden full of it."

Adam tipped his head to the side and chuckled. "Well, just look at it like this: when I finally do have my own little piece of earth where I can plant my garden, I'll be ready to cultivate it and enjoy all the fruits of my years of planning and labor."

"Fine," said Martin. "But if you've got it in mind for my cousin to be your gardenin partner, you might as well get your mind off of that and instead think about all those other things you'll need to do before you ever even think about plantin."

Adam turned beet red, and he threw his palm over his mouth and rubbed at his freshly shaven cheeks to conceal the fact that he was trying hard not to smile. Martin mischievously raised his eyebrows and gave a quick little wink and nod, and made a clicking sound.

Adam didn't say another word until they got to Laney's house. He couldn't stop smiling, but he was too embarrassed to talk. He hoped that Martin wouldn't refer to fruit *or* gardens at the dinner party, or he might just fall right out of his chair.

WHEN THEY FINALLY GOT TO the house and were shown inside by Laney, Adam was impressed with how festive the place was decorated. Candles were lit and boughs of longleaf pine lined the windowsills.

Aunt Celie had spent days preparing everything for a special dinner. Cyrus's wife, Violet, helped her, and they even enlisted Laney and Catherine to take on certain tasks.

"We gon' make a cook outta you, chil', if it's the last thing I do," Aunt Celie had said to Laney, as it was later relayed to Adam.

On the menu for the festive occasion were seafood chowder, venison pie, roast turkey, ham hock–seasoned string beans with boiled potatoes, corn pudding, oyster dressing, and stewed carrots. For dessert Aunt Celie had variety of sweet treats to offer—syllabubs, apple fritters, gingerbread cake, sugar cookies, and blueberry cobbler.

While Adam, Martin, Laney, Will, and Catherine waited for Aunt Celie and Violet to put the finishing touches on the dinner, Will used it as an opportunity to inquire about details regarding Harmon's capture, as well as his expected fate.

Adam explained how everything had transpired the day he returned from Bath. Will then peppered him with questions about everything from his and Martin's trip to New Bern and Bath, to how Adam came to figure out where Harmon had gone, and how he had trapped him.

"I've since learned that he and Reuben weren't brothers at all," said Adam. "It was just part of their charade. I'm told they came from up there in Halifax County."

"Halifax County?" Will said. "Way up there?"

"Mm-hmm." Adam nodded. "I don't know if they've both always been there, but that's where they've spent the most time over the last few years. They've both gotten into all kinds of trouble up there, and around Bertie and Edgecombe Counties, but this little highwaymen scheme was the first time they had ever worked together."

"I reckon that explains why they didn't look a bit alike," said Martin.

"Exactly," Adam agreed. "And apparently they've left a whole string of robbery victims along the way. And the incident up near Handcock and Slocomb Creeks with the Dudleys was not the first murder they'd committed—or maybe I should say it wasn't the first murder Harmon committed. He did kill that shopkeeper in Paxon's scheme. As far as the authorities know, that was the first. At least they've not heard tell of any others that fit the pattern."

"Seems strange that a man would just become a killer like that," Laney remarked. "Robbery is bad enough, but I can't help but wonder what made him turn so evil."

"I would suppose," said Will, "that once Harmon had killed that shopkeeper, it hardened him. Maybe he figured after that he didn't have anything to lose. From there he could carry out whatever wicked scheme his diabolical mind could contrive—robbery, murder, even rape."

"Oh!" gasped Laney. She looked horrified at the thought.

"No doubt his crimes are done with now," said Adam. "You can be sure that when he goes to trial he'll be judged fairly and found guilty. The hangman's noose is the only thing he has to look forward to in the New Year."

"What about the servant girl in New Bern?" Laney asked. "Do they know whether or not Harmon and his accomplice are responsible for that crime?"

"No, they aren't," said Adam. "Penelope Wilson is an apprentice girl, you know, and she had apparently caught the eye of the son of her master. He had taken her in his carriage under the pretext of doing some errand but then attempted to take liberties with the poor girl and left her on the side of the road when she fought back. She had been too scared to tell the authorities who was responsible, but the driver evidently came forward."

Laney's eyes grew huge in shock at that news.

"Gracious!" Catherine winced. "The time cannot come soon enough when we can be done talking about all of this." She put a protective hand over her round belly. "We're bringing a child into this world, Will, and it grieves me terribly to think too much of its wickedness. I'm overwhelmed with worry for the evils that our babe might have to face."

Will tenderly took his wife's hand and smiled in an effort to comfort her. "I understand. The days are evil," he said, "but you know as well as I there's really nothing new under the sun."

Catherine sighed. "I suppose you're right. But still…"

"I'm sorry, ma'am," said Adam. "I'm done talking about all of this. Anyway, it's the Christmas season, so we've got greater things to be thankful for."

"Yes, we do," said Laney.

At that moment Aunt Celie rang a little bell from the dining room to let them all know that the table was ready with the sumptuous repast they had prepared.

After moving into the dining room, they all sat down, Will said the blessing, and they dug in to the feast.

They were all enjoying the meal and light conversation. Adam felt a tremendous sense of relief that everything was well and truly back to normal—and just in time for Christmas.

The previous year, although he and Laney had become better acquainted after the situation with Rasquelle, they still didn't know each other well enough that Laney would invite him to her house for a Christmas supper—even if it was still a few days before Christmas. Here he was, wearing fine clothes—his own, not ones that he had to borrow—and he felt exceedingly thankful that everything was starting to come together.

And then it happened.

Catherine said, "Spring will be here before we know it."

"Indeed," Laney agreed. "And my new little niece or nephew! I can't wait!"

"You know," said Martin, "y'all are right. It does seem like spring gets here in no time after Christmas. It'll soon be time for planting, won't it?"

Adam kicked Martin under the table. Martin just took another bite of string beans and grinned at him.

"Indeed it will," said Catherine. "I've always enjoyed working in the garden—well, the harvesting part, anyway." She laughed. "Have you fellows ever done any gardening?" she asked Adam and Martin.

"Every chance I get," said Martin, before taking a giant bite of a dinner roll.

Adam shook his head. "No, I can't say that I have. I'd like to try it someday, though." Adam grinned at Martin, pleased with himself for adeptly navigating this tricky conversation.

"You really ought to try your hand at it first chance you get," said Catherine. "You might really take to it."

"Oh, I'm sure I will," said Adam. "But Emmanuel still has work for me to do. He keeps me right busy. I don't reckon I'll get to enjoy any gardening until I've finished my apprenticeship and gotten my own little piece of land."

"Oh, Adam," Laney said, "if you ever want to try your hand at planting a garden, you're welcome to come do it here. We've got good, fertile soil."

Adam swallowed hard and discreetly looked at Martin like he would kill him if he said another word.

"You hear that, Fletcher?" said Martin. "You may be well on your way to establishing your own little garden after all."

In a blessed moment of relief, Will changed the subject.

"Adam, tell us. When will you come to New Bern again? I regret the fact your last two visits there were so rushed."

"I'm not sure when," he answered. "I'd like to come back when it's warm out, though. I heard there's a big racing ground north of town. I'd love to see a proper race."

"Come anytime from mid-March onward," said Will. "Saturdays are racing days, so you'll want to plan your visit to include one of those."

Adam nodded enthusiastically. "I'd love that."

"You come, too," Will said to Martin. "I know you love to wager on the horses."

"I thought you said I gamble too much," Martin countered.

"Of course you do," said Laney, "but horse racing is refined. It's a gentleman's sport—not like those awful card games you like to play."

Adam and Martin exchanged glances. They were both thinking about Ed Willis.

Laney must've realized it, because she quickly said, "Oh, I'm sorry."

"It's alright," said Adam.

"Oh, one other thing," said Will. "I've heard Governor Tryon is nearly ready to hire an architect to build his palace in New Bern. And do you know where it will be?"

Adam shook his head.

"Less than a block away from our estate! It will be quite a thing to see such a fine home go up from the ground to completion.

They say it will be a remarkable residence—one of the best in the colonies."

"Wonder what folks in the backcountry will think about all that," Adam said. "I've heard they're already agitated over a lack of any real representation out that way."

"There's no telling," said Will, "but having a proper governor's mansion in New Bern will be good for this region, I am sure of it."

For the rest of the meal they chatted about all kinds of things. Finally, it was time for Adam and Martin to head back into town. Adam would drop Martin off at his home on the way.

Chapter Thirty-Five

WHEN ADAM MADE IT BACK to the warehouse, he was surprised to find his grandfather out of bed and sitting in his chair, reading the paper.

"Are you feeling better?" he asked Emmanuel.

"Well, I'm up anyway," Emmanuel answered.

Adam could see that the old man was doing his best to stay warm, wearing his blue banyan, or house coat, over his layers of clothing, and a gray knit cap on his head. He also had a quilt folded in half over his legs.

"I'm tired of being in bed," he said. "My back and my shoulders and my hands are all aching terribly whether I'm lying down or sitting, so I thought it best to get up and move around a bit into a different position so that my old bones don't lock in place."

"That sounds like a wise thing to do. Can I get you anything?" Adam asked. "Would you like another cup of tea?"

Emmanuel looked into the bone china cup sitting on the little table beside him. He picked it up and took a sip and then said, "No, I don't think so. Thank you. How was the supper at Miss Rocksolonah's home?"

"It was perfect. Everything tasted so good, and there was so much of it."

"And the young lady? How is she?" Emmanuel asked.

"Laney? She's just fine." He smiled. "And beautiful, as always."

"That's wonderful. I'm happy to hear you had a nice time," said Emmanuel. "I was just reading the paper here. Boaz brought it to me this afternoon so I'd have something new to look at."

"Oh good," said Adam. "I reckon it's too soon for them to have anything about the apprehension of Harmon."

"I should think so," said Emmanuel. "But you will want to know that your name is printed right here." He pointed to the top of the far left column on the last page of the paper.

"What in the world for?" he asked.

"It says there is a letter waiting for you at New Bern."

"What? May I see?"

Emmanuel handed him the paper.

"Hmph. It sure does! I've never been sent a letter before. Who in the world would be writing to me?"

His grandfather shrugged. "That I do not know."

"And why would they send it to New Bern?"

"It may have been carried here if it said Carteret next to your name, but as it's written… See there"—he pointed to the paper in Adam's hand—"it says Beaufort. You see some of the places listed beside the names are counties and others are towns. We have a Beaufort County—where Bath is, of course—and a Beaufort town here in Carteret. I would imagine they just weren't sure which it should be."

"Hmm," said Adam. "I don't know what to think about this."

Emmanuel chuckled. "I do. Looks like you'll be traveling again. You've got another mystery to solve."

"I reckon I do," said Adam. "The mystery of who wrote this letter. But with that thunder the other night, snow is coming, so this might have to wait a few weeks."

Emmanuel nodded in agreement.

"Do you mind if I keep this paper? I've never seen my name in the paper before," said Adam.

"Sure you can keep it, but do you mind if I finish reading it first?" Emmanuel held out his hand so that Adam would give him the paper back.

"Oh, of course not," Adam said, handing it to him.

He stood from the settee to excuse himself to go to bed.

Emmanuel turned to the page he had been reading before Adam came in, then looked over his spectacles at his grandson and called out to him, "You know, I'm reminded of something."

Adam turned back to look at him. "What's that?"

"When you first came here, I remember you said you had never been anywhere. You couldn't wait to go to new places, see new things. Seventeen years old you were, and you'd never even left Carteret County. Just look at you now—you've been to New Bern more than once, Bath, Nassau, and even Havana. Seems you've gone far in a short time. Wonder where else you'll go?"

Adam took a deep breath in contemplation, then let out a sigh. "You're right. I have been to a lot of places in a short time, but I'll tell you one thing."

"What's that?"

"This place—Carteret County—this will always be home. And there's no place else I'd rather be."

Emmanuel smiled. "I'm perfectly happy to hear that, son. Now go to bed, and try to think about who might've sent you that correspondence."

"Oh, believe me I will," said Adam. "Good night."

"Good night."